"Magically delicious! Darynda Jones knocks it out of the park with Betwixt. If you love Charley, you're going to be be obsessed with Defiance. Hilarious, heartwarming and oh so addictive."

-Robyn Peterman ~ NYT and USA Today Bestselling Author

"Darynda Jones brings her original style to paranormal women's fiction, and I for one couldn't be happier. Also, maybe be wary of inheriting from strangers...or not. Go get this book!"

—Michelle M. Pillow, New York Times and USA Today Bestselling Author of the Warlocks MacGregor series

"Betwixt takes readers on a heartwarming, spellbinding journey packed full of intrigue. Ms. Jones has outdone herself with this gem."

-Mandy M. Roth, NY Times & USA TODAY Bestselling Author

BETWIXT

BETWIXT & BETWEEN BOOK ONE

DARYNDA JONES

This is a work of fiction. All of the characters, organizations, and events portrayed in this novel are either products of the author's imagination or are used fictitiously.

BETWIXT: A PARANORMAL WOMEN'S FICTION NOVEL

(BETWIXT & BETWEEN BOOK 1)

© 2020 by Darynda Jones

Cover design by TheCoverCollection

ISBN 10: 1-7343852-4-3

ISBN 13: 978-1-7343852-4-3

www.DaryndaJones.com

Available in ebook, print, and audio editions

*For those of you who, like me, still believe in magic
even though we're of a certain age.
Stay fierce.*

ONE

There are two kinds of people in the world:
those who believe in magic
and those who are wrong.

I pulled to a stop in front of a sprawling mansion, checked the address the lawyer gave me, then glanced at the mansion again, even more confused than I'd been when I first got the call. No way was this legit. I looked at the numbers on the massive white columns and compared them to the numbers I'd scribbled on a hot pink sticky note. Perfect match. It was one thing for a complete stranger to bequeath me a house. It was quite another for that house to look like a red brick version of Tara from *Gone with the Wind*.

I turned my head to look at the street sign one more time, making sure it said Chestnut, before checking the address a third time. Still a perfect match. Maybe I heard it wrong. Or wrote it down wrong. Or I'd entered the *Twilight Zone*. As I sat steeping in a light marinade of seasonal herbs

and bewilderment, weighing my options—medication, elec-
troshock therapy, exorcism—an urgent knock sounded on
the window of my vintage mint green Volkswagen Beetle,
a.k.a., the bug. I jumped in response, the movement quite
possibly dislocating a rib.

A feminine voice shrieked at me as though the barrier
between us was a concrete wall instead of a piece of glass.
"Ms. Dayne?"

I put an arm around my ribcage to protect it from any
further damage and turned to the panic-stricken woman
enveloped from head to toe in neon purple.

"Hi!" she shouted.

Seriously, every article of clothing she wore—beret,
scarf, wool coat, knitted mittens—were all a shade of purple
so bright my pupils had to adjust.

"Are you Ms. Dayne?"

And I liked purple. Really, I did. Just not a shade so
bright it made my eyes water. Not unlike pepper spray. Or
napalm.

I cracked the window and gave a cautious, "Mrs.
Richter?"

The woman shoved her mitted hand into the narrow
opening I'd created. "So nice to meet you. What do you
think?"

I took her hand a microsecond before she snatched it
back and stepped to the side to allow me to exit.

Mrs. Richter, a woman only a couple of years older than
my own forty-four years of hard labor with little reward,
hurried to the hood of the bug and pulled a stack of papers
from a manila envelope. A stack of papers that probably
needed my signature.

A needlelike cramp tightened the muscles in my stomach. This was all happening too fast. Much like my life of late.

After the first wave of pain subsided—the same pain I'd been having for months now—I pushed a wind-blown lock of black hair over my ear and followed her.

"Mrs. Richter, I don't understand any of this. Why would someone I don't know leave me a house? Especially one that looks straight out of Architectural Digest."

"What?" She glanced up from her task of wrangling the paperwork in the icy wind and let her gaze bounce from the house to me then back to the house. "Oh, heavens. I'm so sorry. Mrs. Goode didn't leave you *this* house. I just wanted to meet here because her house is, well—" She cleared her throat and tried to tame a strand of blond hair that whipped across her forehead. "It's persnickety."

Relief flooded every cell in my body. Either that or the Adderall I'd had in lieu of breakfast was finally kicking in. Still, how in the Sam Spade could a house be persnickety?

Deciding that was a question for another day, I released a breath I didn't know I'd been holding. "That's actually a bit of a weight off my shoulders. There's no way I could afford the taxes and insurance on this place, much less the upkeep."

"Oh, well, that shouldn't be a problem. Somehow the taxes on Percival are stuck in the fifties. Cheapest on the block, but you didn't hear that from me. Also, there's the money that Mrs. Goode—"

"Percival?"

She leaned into the bone-chilling breeze, and whispered, "The house."

I whispered back, "The house is named Percival?"

"Yes." She stopped as though startled, then said, "My goodness, your eyes are beautiful."

"Thank you. Did you say the house—?"

"I don't think I've ever seen that shade of blue before."

"Oh. Um, thanks?"

"You're welcome. Can you sign here, please?" She recovered and pointed to a highlighted spot on the first of many, many pages, clearly in a hurry to get on with it.

I eyed the paper with a suspicion born of far too many deceptive relationships. "How about we go inside and talk about this?"

Her face, a face that had been rosy not thirty seconds earlier, paled at my suggestion. She backed away as though I'd just told her I was going to murder her and keep her heart in a jar on my desk.

I would never do such a thing. I'd keep it in a jar in the cupboard. I wasn't morbid.

"Inside?" She clasped the papers to her chest and took another step back. "You mean, inside Percival?"

I lifted a shoulder. "Sure. Is he, maybe, around here somewhere?"

Her hazel irises glazed over despite the wind whipping her blond bob around her head, beret be damned, and her gaze traveled across the street to land on a structure there. Mine followed.

Towering between two gorgeous houses that were almost as majestic as the one I'd parked in front of sat a huge, crumbling abode. It was gorgeous and grotesque and mesmerizing and I was certain I'd seen it in a horror movie. Or five.

And I was lost.

Percival was gorgeous. Hauntingly beautiful with ivy-covered moss green brick and black trim so dark it looked like wet ink. It sat three stories high. The main section was round with six black gables that formed a circle. Two bay windows graced the front on either side of a massive black door. Another section, square but just as stunning, was attached on the right of it. A tall iron fence surrounded the property with a veritable forest from what I could see of the back.

I didn't want to just live in Percival. I wanted to marry him and have his babies.

Mrs. Richter jerked her gaze away from my future ex-house and back to the bug where she started fighting the wind to straighten the papers again.

Percival certainly left an impression. So had the lawyer who'd insisted over the phone that I drive all the way from Arizona—mostly because a last-minute plane ticket cost more than my car—to the infamous town of Salem, Mass-achusetts—a town I'd never visited—so that she could sign over a house that a woman—a woman I'd never met—left to me. And because I was recently divorced, utterly bankrupt, and just desperate enough to fall for even the most hair-brained scheme, I did it.

Thank God that nice Prince from Algiers who kept promising to send me a million dollars for a small processing fee hadn't called again. I would probably have fallen for that as well.

Instead, I was standing in one of the most famous towns in history, in one of the most beautiful neighbor-hoods I'd ever seen, on one of the iciest days I'd ever felt, talking to one of the strangest women I'd ever met. And I'd met some strange ones. No shortage of those in the A-Z.

"Was it on fire at some point?" I noticed a section of the brick was darker as though it had once been covered in smoke. When I didn't get an answer, I finally took note of Mrs. Richter's pallor which, even in the frigid wind, was bluer than it should have been. "Mrs. Richter, are you okay?"

Keeping her back to Percival, she straightened her shoulders, and said, "It doesn't like me looking at it."

I glanced back at the house. "Percival?"

"Yes. Like I said, it's very persnickety."

Before I could comment, a gust of wind blew several sheets of papers out of her hand.

A high-pitch shriek I didn't know was humanly possible erupted out of her small frame. She bolted forward and chased them down a street dampened with morning dew and fog, all the while screaming, "Oh, God no! Please, God no!"

I did the same, minus the screams. Girl had spunk. Sure she was a mess of frazzled nerves, and it was apparently all Percival's fault, but she could move when she had to.

We zigzagged down the street, lunging after this page or that, and all I could think about was the fact that I hadn't run this much since Brad Fitzpatrick chased me into the boy's locker room in the seventh grade. Also, the fact that we had to look ridiculous.

Mostly the fact that we had to look ridiculous.

Just when I felt a page land between my fingers, it would slip away with the next gust. That was pretty much the process for a good three minutes until the wind started spinning around us. It created a tiny vortex, a whirlwind circling us, and the papers flew inside of it long enough for us to finally grab them. It continued until we had every last one.

My hair would never be the same, but I couldn't have Mrs. Richter stroking out mere minutes after we met. At our age, that was a real possibility.

By the time we got back to the bug, each of us looking

like we'd just come off a drunken bender, I felt so bad for the woman I did the unthinkable. I signed. Every. Single. Page. That is, after she proved there were no liens on the house, no back taxes. Basically, there was no catch.

No catch.

I didn't get it. There had to be a catch. How could there not be?

I held fast to the knowledge that I would have three days to call all of this off. Wasn't there a law to that effect? I would have three days to back out of the deal, no questions asked?

Then I could go back to my shambolic, bankrupt, nigh homeless life since I was currently being evicted from my apartment. I could feel confident in the fact that I did not owe a fortune on a money pit that was going to take me for every cent I didn't have, no matter how alluring said money pit was.

I couldn't believe that at more than four decades on this earth I was an almost homeless has-been. My ex saw to that. Or, well, his mother saw to it. Erina Julson was the most heartless, conniving woman I'd ever met, and still I married her son.

I thought he was different. I thought she no longer had any influence over him. I thought we were in love. I thought wrong. On all counts. They took me for everything I had and then some.

And Annette, my BFF, wondered why I had trust issues.

Yet here I was, possibly making the second biggest mistake of my life. I only had my honor left. My word. My reputation. If I failed again, I wouldn't even have that. Yet I signed.

Thankfully, the more I signed, the more the wind

calmed around us. By the time I handed her back the stack of papers, the neighborhood was as serene as a glass lake.

After replacing the documents in the envelope, she shoved her card toward me with a shaking hand. "Here's my information if you need anything."

I studied it with a mixture of confusion and skepticism. "The number is blacked out."

"Yes, that's right. Please don't call." She stuffed the envelope into her oversized purse, then added, "Ever." She started backing toward her car.

"What if I have questions? Do I just go by your office?"

"No!" She cleared her throat and began again. "I mean, of course. Though I really have no further information on the house itself. I can't imagine why you'd need to."

Damn it. There was a catch. There had to be. "Wait!" I called out to her as she sprinted to a parked purple crossover down the street.

She waved a hand. "My assistant will bring by a copy of the paperwork this afternoon!" Then she dove inside her car and floored it, spinning the front tires in her effort to leave Percival—and me—in her rearview as quickly as possible.

I didn't even know they made purple crossovers.

I glanced at the zippered bag she'd handed me somewhere between the tornado and her nickel-slick getaway, wondering once again if I'd just made the biggest mistake of my life.

She'd had no answers for me over the phone and apparently that hadn't changed.

"I don't understand," I'd told her when she called three days ago. "Someone left me a house?"

"Yes. Free and clear. It's all yours. Mrs. Goode left explicit instructions in her will and I promised her—"

"I'm sorry. I don't know a Ruthie Goode. There must be a mistake."

"She said you'd say that."

"Mrs. Richter, people don't just leave strangers houses."

"She said you'd say that, too."

"Not to mention the fact that I live in Arizona. I've never even been to Massachusetts."

"And that. I don't know what to tell you, sweetheart. Mrs. Goode left very detailed instructions. You must accept the house in person within the next seventy-two hours to take possession. Either way, it cannot be sold to anyone else for a year. If you don't take it, it'll just sit there, abandoned and vulnerable."

Abandoned and vulnerable. No words in the English language made me more uncomfortable.

Three days.

Well, maybe syphilis.

I had three days to decide.

And moist.

I turned to the abode known as Percival, took another good look at what a woman I'd never met named Ruthie Goode left me, then climbed back into the bug and pulled her into Percival's driveway.

My life had been punctuated by the strange and unexplained. I was flypaper for what others called the weird. Countless friends and coworkers had remarked on the fact that if there was an unstable sentient being within a ten-mile radius, it would find its way to me eventually. Dog. Cat. Woman. Man. Iguana.

I once had to track down the parents of a toddler who thought I was her dead aunt Lucille. An aunt she'd never met, according to the aforementioned procreators.

Everyone called these admirers, for lack of a better term, weird. I called them charming. Quirky. Eccentric.

This, however, took the raspberry covered chocolate cheesecake. I'd only been bequeathed one other item from a departed member of society, and that was when Greg Sanchez handed me his half-eaten ice cream cone seconds before falling into a volcano.

That field trip did not end well.

I grabbed my overnight bag and paused again to get a better look at Percival.

He was already growing on me, damn him. I had a thing for the broody ones. The dark ones with deep, invisible scars who looked like they'd fought a thousand battles. Percival definitely fit the bill.

Filling my lungs with crisp New England air, air that held the smoky scent of wood burning from hearths nearby, I stepped to Percy's front door, took the key out of the zippered bag Mrs. Richter had given me, and entered.

I stopped just inside the foyer so Percy and I could chat. "Okay, Percy," I said aloud, only feeling a little silly. "Do you mind if I call you Percy?" I let my eyes adjust to the dimness inside the house. "Looks like it's just you and me."

Of course, the moment I said that, a black cat, who looked like it had been through a few battles itself, rushed past my ankles and leapt up the stairs as though its tail were on fire. I let out a squeak that could summon a pod of dolphins and hurried to close the door before any other creatures of the forest decided to join us.

Then I turned to get the full effect of what Percy had to offer.

Even though Mrs. Goode had passed only three days prior, someone had thoughtfully covered the furniture with white sheets. Yet every surface was covered in dust and a legion of spiders had set up shop in the corners and along the walls, if their silvery snares were any indication. It made the house even eerier.

Floorboards squeaked as I took in the dusty wood floors and deep gray walls. Even the ceilings were covered with the charcoal color, including the decorative crown moldings and graceful, spider-webbed arches.

I took a careful step closer to the great room. It was huge with identical staircases on either side leading up to a common landing. Though the sheen may have worn off him, Percival had been stunningly glamorous in his time. A good scrubbing and a few hundred gallons of paint and who knew what he could be again?

Walking inside this monolith was like nothing I'd ever felt before. A rush of adrenaline slid through me, leaving no cell untouched. A lulling calmness followed. Along with a sense of nostalgia, which made no sense. I would've remembered something this lonely and beautiful, and I'd never set foot outside of Arizona before three days ago.

Percy felt it too. After an initial shudder of distrust, he seemed to settle around me like a warm cloak. A really warm cloak.

I realized he was hot. Too hot, especially since no one besides Mrs. Goode had lived here, according to the purple people eater. The house should be empty. Who'd kept the heat on?

My phone rang, the tinny sound out of place in such a marvelous tribute to days gone by.

I pressed the green dot and answered with a, "You are not going to believe this place."

My bestie ignored me. "What I can't believe is the fact that your rust bucket of a vehicle made it."

Annette Osmund had been my best friend since we'd

taken Coach Teague's Intro to Biology in high school together. It was her mop of curly brown hair and red cat-eye glasses that initially drew me to her. It was her bizarre oxymoronic person-ality—irreverent yet warm—that'd kept me coming back for more. We'd had an instant connection, as though our souls knew we would still be best friends over twenty-five years later.

I walked into a side room. A room my predecessor might have called a sitting room or a drawing room. I'd read enough historical romance novels to be downright giddy, the emotion racing along my spine and sparking out to my fingertips.

"Rust bucket?" I asked, appalled. "You mean my vintage mint green Volkswagen Beetle?"

"Stop."

I stifled a giggle. "What? Do you have something against my vintage mint green Volkswagen Beetle?"

"I'm not kidding."

"You don't respect her. What has my vintage mint green Volkswagen Beetle ever done to you?"

"I swear to God, Dephne, if you say vintage mint green Volkswagen Beetle one more time."

"Vintage mint green Volkswagen Beetle one more time. When does your plane land?"

"Never. I'm abandoning you in your hour of need."

I stopped short, my fingertips lingering on a delicately carved piece of molding. "You know you can be replaced."

She snorted. "No, I can't."

"I have other people in my life."

"No, you don't."

"Several of whom could easily be promoted to sidekick."

"Not true."

"You hold that position very precariously."

"No— Okay, that's quite likely."

I did a 360, dizzy with joy and inspiration and a sickly sense of dread. Even if I could keep the house, I could never afford to give it the attention it so desperately needed. It simply wasn't meant to be.

"This house is gorgeous, Nette. It's ancient and dank and dusty, yet it has so much potential."

"Like your vagina?"

"What's strange is that, even though Mrs. Goode only passed away three days ago, it's like no one has entered it in years."

"Oh, then it's *exactly* like your vagina."

She spoke softly to her pharmacist, a.k.a. her barista, as I walked through a maze of connecting rooms. I ended up in an industrial kitchen. Part of it was so outdated, it was downright historical. The other part of it looked brand new with appliances I would have killed for in my restaurant. It was an odd mix of old and new and every inch of it was wonderful.

"I'll have you know," I said, when she came back online, "my vagina has been entered many times over the years." I stopped to get a better look at a woodburning stove that clearly hadn't been used in years. I'd never seen one in real life.

"Mmm-hmm."

"Many, many times."

"So has my Barbie Dreamhouse."

I gasped. "Are you comparing my vagina to your Barbie Dreamhouse?"

"Pretty much. Both are about as useful in the real world."

My vagina had never been so insulted in her entire

vaginal life. "She has been entered plenty. More times than the Taj Mahal."

"Good to know."

"More times than the US."

"Who are you trying to convince?"

I gestured wildly, pointing at nothing in particular. "My vagina has been entered more times than a Kardashian's pin number."

"Keep talking, Snow White."

Oh, that was the last straw. "Listen here, Miss My-Love-Life's-Better-Than-Yours. A plethora of men have entered my vagina. Dozens. Possibly hundreds." My voice rose with each syllable. "Many a warrior has stormed these gates and come back the better man for it. Don't even think about worrying your pretty little head about my special place. What you should be worrying about is—"

I stopped talking the moment I turned and spotted a tall, shirtless man with more ink than the *New York Times* standing in, purportedly, *my* kitchen. He was drying his hands on a towel, staring me down. Much like I was doing to him. Minus the towel.

TWO

Guys,
gray in the beard is sexy.
Leave it alone.
Thank you,
-Grown Ass Women

In all honesty, I had about a thousand more reasons to stare than he did. He was unkempt and scruffy and startlingly handsome. The kind of handsome that forces perusers to pause on a page in a magazine while absently thumbing through it. As though they had no choice. As though the glint in his eyes had demanded their attention.

In a word, he was stunning. Because nothing short of stunning would give me pause in this particular situation. I had never, in all of my forty-plus years, thought a possible intruder handsome. The mind didn't work that way. If it did, survival of the fittest would be a moot point. All of Darwin's work for naught.

Then again, it could have been the kilt.

I absorbed every aspect of the man in a matter of seconds. Dark red hair streaked with gold brushed shoulders wide enough to carry the world. A short beard, only a shade lighter than his hair and tinted with a silvery-gray, framed a perfectly formed face. A lean body, clearly sculpted by Michelangelo, stood solid and unabashed.

And then, of course, the kilt.

Holy mother of God. It was made of a dark, thin leather, the jagged edges coming to a stop at mid-calf, a few inches above a pair of work boots.

Add to that the fact that he'd been bathed in ink, and I was a goner. Full sleeves. Stenciled hands. Archaic symbols cropping up one side of his neck.

But the *pièce de résistance* was a giant black and gray skull that spanned the entire length of his torso, its dark eyes almost as penetrating as the man's olive-green ones. The same ones that shimmered beneath dark lashes as he studied me.

After an eternity of two distinct emotions battling for dominion—fear and utter, soul-crushing humiliation due to the vagina monologue—fear won out.

It usually did.

I grabbed a wedge of wood off the stove and jabbed it toward him. "Stay back! I have 9-1-1 on the phone."

An easy grin lifted one corner of his mouth, the slow movement almost dropping me. "Discussing your special place?" he asked with a voice straight out of an aged bottle of bourbon.

My stomach flip-flopped, even though now was not the time for acrobatics. Now was the time for stealth. For wile and cunning. I had to prepare to fight him. Or run.

Probably run.

I blinked, my mind racing to come up with a plausible explanation as to why I would be talking to the cops about my vagina. A justification that would convince this heathen intruder I had 5-o mere seconds away.

I stabbed him with my best glare and said, "Y—yes."

That'd do it.

He'd be hightailing it out of here any moment now.

He continued to wipe his hands on the towel, his gaze never wavering from mine.

Any moment.

Instead, he spoke again. His voice disarmingly similar to the butterscotch whiskey my dads made the summer I turned twenty-one. Sweet and rich and so intoxicating I vomited for two days. I realized later they were using aversion therapy. It didn't work.

He gestured toward my hand with a nod. "That's not what you think it is."

I frowned at him, not sure what he meant until he looked at the wedge of wood I'd been holding onto for dear life.

Realization dawned and I dropped it in horror before examining my hand like it had just been exposed to Ebola, careful to keep it away from the rest of me.

Where was my hazmat suit when I needed it?

I fought my gag reflex as I scanned the room in a frenzied panic, hoping to find a bottle of dish soap. Or bleach. Or battery acid.

"It's still not what you think it is," he said with a soft chuckle.

Oh, thank God. I calmed and dropped my hand. "Then what—?"

"Coffee?"

That was coffee? I looked at the briquette I just dropped. "I didn't know coffee would do that."

He turned to get a burnt umber T-shirt that lay atop a small breakfast table, and I got a good look at the tattoos on his shoulders and back. A large symbol rested on his spine, like something from an ancient language. It sat superimposed on a map I recognized immediately because I'd been studying the town at night when I'd stop to get what little sleep I could in my car. It was an early map of Salem, most likely drawn around the 1600s.

It was the symbol that called to me, however. Drew me closer, and I took an involuntary step toward him. Though I recognized it, its meaning lay hidden behind a thick curtain. Like a word that rested on the tip of my tongue and refused to fully form.

Unfortunately, he made quick work of donning the T-shirt. The hem settled softly around his kilt-clad hips, an inch above the swell of what promised to be a rock-hard ass. I came to the realization that I'd never been so attracted to a man in my entire life.

I dragged my gaze down to his left leg before I did something we'd both regret. Just above the boot, a scar snaked up from underneath the top, and I wondered what had happened to him.

When he took two cups down from a cabinet, I realized there was a coffee pot not ten feet away from me.

"Oh, right. Coffee."

"Would you like a cup?"

Before I could answer, I heard a screeching sound coming from my phone and almost dropped it trying to get it back to my ear. "Sorry . . . officer. It's okay. I thought there was an intruder."

There was an intruder, but he'd offered me coffee, so we were practically besties.

"Intruder my ass," Annette said. "He sounds hot. What does he look like?"

"I couldn't possibly say at the moment, but thank you for your call."

"Oh, come on. Give me a hint."

"I'll be sure to send in my donation to the Policemen's None of Your Business Foundation."

"Don't you even think about hanging up on—"

I ended the call and turned back to Ginger Spice. Caffeine normally calmed me down. Ever since I got the call about the house, however, nothing seemed to work. I'd been running on all cylinders for three days.

"I would love some. My first three cups don't seem to have done the trick, but before we exchange friendship bracelets . . ." I cleared my throat. "Who are you again?"

"Roane." He turned back to me and held out his hand. "Roane Wildes. You must be Ms. Dayne." His hand swallowed mine a split second before he went back to the task at hand. There was something about the way he said *Ms. Dayne* that sent goose bumps racing over my skin.

"How do you know that?"

He passed me a cup and gestured toward a carton of cream and a bowl of sugar that sat beside the pot, the bowl as aged and delicate as the house in which it resided. "Ruthie told me."

"Mrs. Goode? You spoke to her?"

"Mrs. Goode?" he asked, as though confused. Then he corrected himself. "Of course. She told me you didn't know. I spoke to her every chance I got. She was a captivating mixture of class and mystery. I'm sorry for your loss."

I sat down and tore my gaze off him to look out into the

massive wooded backyard. I didn't want to come across as creepy. His words startled me. I glanced up at him. "I didn't know her."

He sat down, his face betraying the sadness he clearly felt at Mrs. Goode's passing. "I helped her out when I could. Mostly just fixing this or that. I'm a journeyman. Though she knew pretty much everyone in town, she didn't have anyone to help with the little things."

"That's very kind of you. You seem to have been close to her."

"I was."

"If she only passed a few days ago, why does the house look like it hasn't been lived in for months?"

He dipped his head and took a slow sip. "She got sick. She didn't have the energy to take care of Percival and mostly stayed in her room on the second floor."

He called the house Percival, too. I guess that made it official.

"If I'd known how sick she was, I would've helped." His face softened as he thought of her.

"Was she—? Were you related?"

"No. Just . . . friends."

"I'm so sorry for your loss."

"Thank you. It happened so fast, I think I'm still processing."

My heart ached for him. "Roane, do you know why she would leave me the house? I mean, I didn't know her. Though, admittedly, I was adopted when I was three. I don't remember anything before that. I do know my birth parents were from Arizona. Were we somehow related?"

"I think I should let her explain."

I'd started to take another sip but put the cup down again. "I don't understand."

He stood, walked to a jacket that hung on the doorknob to the backyard, and took an envelope out of the pocket. "She left this for you." He walked back and handed it to me. "It should shed some light onto what's going on."

I opened it, my movements wary. I wasn't sure how much I wanted to know now that it was all happening. The envelope contained a note with a URL written on it, the penmanship beautiful.

"I'm supposed to go here?"

"Yeah. She recorded a message for you before she died. She didn't want you to have it unless . . . unless she passed. It's on a file at that address."

"Thank you." I stared at the address as though it might hold all the answers I'd been searching for.

"I feel like I know all about your vagina," he said, bringing me back to the present, "but very little about you."

A heat comparable to a nuclear blast rushed over my skin. I could only imagine the shades of red I was turning, which made my face even hotter. "Yeah, sorry about that. I thought I was alone."

"Don't apologize. I enjoyed the conversation." That grin reappeared and a wave of heat washed over me again, this time for a different reason.

"It's really warm in here," I said, unbuttoning my jacket.

"Which is why I'm working on the furnace today. Percival can be a jerk."

Right. He was a journeyman. "Look, about that. I appreciate your help, but I can't afford you right now."

I couldn't even afford a hotel room at the moment. I hadn't been this broke since my ramen-noodle college days. I didn't want to call my dads, to drag them into the quagmire that was my life. I'd made my bed. Unfortunately, it had been with a thieving snake. An imposter who'd convinced me I could have my happily ever after if I just signed my name here. And here. Oh, and here.

I tried giving up signing my name on anything ever again. Unfortunately, the world didn't work that way.

"Not a problem," Roane said. "I'm all paid up." He stood and gestured toward the stairs. "Ruthie's room is upstairs on the second floor, first room on the right. The sheets are clean and the water is hot. You look like you could use some rest."

I cringed. "That bad, huh?" I hadn't showered in three days. Apparently, it showed.

Roane shook his head. "Bad is not the word I'd use."

Remembering the creature that'd slipped past me, I said, "Oh, there's a cat."

"Yeah, sorry about that. His name is Ink. Short for Incognito."

"He was Ruthie's?"

"No, he's mine. Though I'd appreciate it if you didn't tell anyone. He causes more trouble in the neighborhood than a gang of rabid raccoons. Also, he hates everyone, so you shouldn't see him much. If you do, just kick him out."

"Does he have food here? Just in case?"

An easy smile slid across his face. "He'll be fine."

After offering to help me get settled, which I declined, Roane went back to work and I brought my bag inside. I took the stairs to the second floor and looked out over the balcony into the foyer. This place was breathtaking.

Though I loathed the thought of sleeping in Ruthie's room, apparently it was the only one with an actual bed. The other rooms, all thirteen of them, were empty. Annette would have to sleep with me when she arrived in the morning. For now, I just wanted a shower. Sleep could wait, even though I'd hardly gotten any for the last three days. Every time I closed my lids, I dreamed of wolves.

A wolf, actually.

I would only catch glimpses of the beautiful creature. Red with a black undercoat. Because of that, sleep had been evasive.

The room, like the rest of the house, had rich, black walls and floor-to-ceiling windows. The bathroom, however, was bright. Light gray wallpaper and white fixtures with a claw-foot tub that called my name like a siren in the night. Not a police siren either.

After an incredible shower, I crawled onto Ruthie's four-poster bed, fought the urge to dive under the blankets, and opened my laptop. I searched the Wi-Fi options, assuming I'd have to use the hotspot on my phone. But one name on the network caught my eye: Defiance.

I clicked on it and was connected instantly. Did Ruthie know I would come? Was she that confident I'd show? Of course, the words *free house* would probably lure someone in WITSEC out of hiding.

I typed in the URL. A box popped up asking me if I wanted to download the file. Figuring I had nothing else to lose, I said yes just as my stomach growled.

I double-clicked on the file, fully prepared to lose my entire life as I'd likely just downloaded a virus, and watched as several folders loaded. One in particular captured my attention. Just like the connection, it was named Defiance. I clicked on it and a video popped onto the screen.

A woman with shoulder-length blond hair appeared. I instantly hit pause. A solid white background did nothing to indicate where she was and I had no idea if she'd filmed the video three days ago or three years.

The woman I'd assumed was Ruthie Goode was so

much more elegant than I'd imagined she would be. I hadn't known what to expect, but a disposition born of nobility had not been it.

It was the tilt of her chin. The firmness of her mouth. The confidence in her eyes. She was poise and grace and she was beautiful.

Seriously, was everything in this town stunning? Percival. Roane. And now Ruthie Goode.

The cat jumped on the bed just then, proving my theory wrong, and sauntered his way toward me as though doing me a favor. Ink may not have been as stunningly gorgeous as the aforementioned, but even he had a certain scruffy charm. A street-hardened charisma.

Like much of the house, he was black, only he had tufts of hair missing and a scar across his face. Part of one ear was gone and his olive-green irises were relaxed yet alert. I got the feeling he didn't miss much.

"You've seen more than your fair share of battles, haven't you, mister?"

I scratched his ears, mostly because he let me, and clicked play again.

Ruthie blinked at the screen as though surprised, cleared her throat, and began. "Defiance," she said, her voice husky like a lounge singer in a smoke-filled bar. "You don't know me. I'm your grandmother."

I sucked in a soft breath. I'd always wondered about my heritage. Where I'd come from. What my biological parents had been like. And now, after all these years, it seemed like I would finally get some answers. Suddenly, I was ten again, questioning everything. Hoping to have been loved. Praying I hadn't been discarded like yesterday's paper. but cherished. Given up for a good reason.

"It's a long story," she continued, her eyes glistening

with moisture, "and I know you have questions, there are just some things we have to do before we can get to that. For now, I'll just say that . . . your mother died when you were three."

No. A hand covered my mouth as something inside me broke. A dream. A childish fantasy I'd had since I was a little girl. If Mrs. Goode were to be believed, I would never get to meet the woman who bore me. The woman whom I always believed had let me go. She'd had no other choice.

"I'm sorry that you're learning of her death this way. I wanted to find you. To tell you everything and bring you home, but I made a promise, and I've done everything in my power to keep it."

A promise? What kind of promise would keep a grandmother from seeking out her granddaughter?

"As far as your father goes, your mother never told me his name. I have no idea who he was."

Wow. I couldn't decide if I was disappointed or elated. He could still be alive. He could still be out there, but if no records of him existed, there was no way I could find him.

I hit pause again and studied her. My grandmother. She had Prussian blue eyes like mine. That was the only resemblance I could find as my hair was as dark as the walls around me and grace lived in a land far, far away.

My stomach growled again. I needed food and rest and time to process everything. I closed my laptop and went in search of Roane. To my surprise, Ink followed me, keeping a safe distance away from my feet. I knew he was smart.

After calling out for Roane and searching for him throughout Percival's exquisite entirety, I decided to order enough pizza for him in case he showed up again. And how could I not order it from The Flying Saucer Pizza Company? With a name like that, it had to be good. When the doorbell rang, I thought it was said pizza. It was not. It was Mrs. Richter's assistant.

"Hi," I said when I opened the door. His pallor told me he was scared of Percival as well. I didn't get it. Percy had been so nice to me. Welcoming.

Without uttering a word, the stout man with chubby cheeks extended his arm to hand me the package, clearly worried Percy was going to bite.

"Thanks." I took the thick envelope, and asked, "So, I have three days to back out of all of this, right? I mean, if I change my mind? Isn't that, like, a law?"

He took a wary step back and I could see a bead of sweat forming on his upper lip. "Three days?"

"Yeah. You know. Isn't there a lemon law or something?"

Another step. "You want to give it back after three days?"

"Okay," I said, walking onto the porch and closing the door behind me. "What gives? What's going on? I mean, it's just a house. A gorgeous, elegant house that needs a little TLC, but a house nonetheless."

The man backed onto the first step. "Nothing. There's nothing wrong with it."

"Then what? Why is everyone so freaked out about Percival?"

He took another step down. "Freaked out? Wh—what makes you say that?"

I gave him my best deadpan. "Seriously?"

After almost stumbling on the next step, he righted himself, then said, "It's just, well, you're not from here. Things have happened in this house. Strange dinner parties happening at all hours of the night. Séances. Mass murders."

"Yeah, we have those in Arizona, too. They're called urban legends."

A nervous chuckled bubbled out of him. "Right. Urban legends. Well, good luck."

He turned and speed walked away. It would have been funny if I hadn't been so concerned. Strange dinner parties happening at all hours of the night? No way could I stay here now. Not with the threat of strange dinner parties happening at all hours of the night.

Speaking of which, the UberEats girl arrived with the pizza. I tipped her with my last five, wondering if I should've used that money more wisely. I could not believe it. I was going to have to borrow a couple hundred bucks from my dads just to get home unless I made a sale on Etsy lickety-split. I made custom journals in my spare time, time being a commodity I seemed to have a lot of lately. Those journals made me a solid twelve bucks a month. Can't shake a stick at that.

After a nasty divorce in which no one besides my ex's mother came out ahead, I'd been wallowing in misery at home, trying to devise a plan of action so I wouldn't starve to death, when I got the call from Mrs. Richter.

And here I stood. Pockets empty. Pizza in hand. Cat around ankles. I'd never owned a cat in my life, but if an ink-covered journeyman came with him, I could learn to love the scruffy little guy.

Since that journeyman was nowhere to be found and Ink was trying to summon a demon with all of the meowing he was doing, obviously wanting the pizza more than I did, I took it upstairs and we ate on the bed. I could only hope Ruthie wouldn't curse me from the grave for getting crumbs on her deep gray comforter.

While eating, I took out my fine-tooth comb and

scoured the paperwork, looking for any indication that accepting this house would break me financially. Then I remembered, one had to actually have finances for them to be broken.

I was no lawyer—though I did represent myself in traffic court once, #neveragain—but the paperwork *looked* legit. Of course, so did the marriage license Lionel Corte gave me in the second grade before he proposed. If I'd known it was fake and we weren't really married, I wouldn't have put him in a sleeper hold. So, in a way, his subsequent aversion to marriage was his own fault.

Like Mrs. Richter said, there didn't seem to be any liens or outstanding taxes, but still, a house like this took lots of dead presidents to maintain. Even more if I was going to consider restoring it.

My phone rang with a video call. I answered it on my laptop and waited for my two dads to appear on the screen.

"Hey, Dad. Hey, Papi." To keep them straight, I'd given them different terms of endearment when I was a kid. I didn't even realize until later that I'd mixed them up. Dad was of Latino descent, his skin a rich copper, the angles of his face sharply defined, while Papi was pure Viking.

"You were supposed to call us the minute you arrived, cariña," Dad said.

"I'm sorry. This has been such a strange day."

They glanced at each other, their handsome faces lined with concern.

My dads had been together for almost fifty years and had been married since Arizona legalized same-sex marriages in 2014. They were more rugged than most straight men. They also had more women hit on them than most straight men, especially men of their age. They were like those silver-fox models in sunglasses ads.

Dad, the older of the two, had silver hair and a cropped, well-groomed beard to match.

Papi, who was almost ten years Dad's junior, was still fighting tooth and nail to keep his dark blond locks dark blond. Sadly, he'd been losing the battle for years now. We'd tried to convince him the gray looked good. We had yet to succeed.

They'd adopted me when I was three, so it wasn't like I didn't have good role models. It wasn't like I didn't know the difference between a good man and a jerk. Yet I married the definition of a conniving snake. He'd fooled me completely.

He hadn't fooled them, though.

"What do you think of the house?" Papi asked. They seemed nervous. Jumpy.

"I think I can't keep it. It's so beautiful. You guys would love it. I just can't afford it."

"Wait, what about—" He stopped when Dad elbowed him. With a stiff nod, he cleared his throat, and said, "Just sleep on it, hon. We can help."

"What's going on?"

"What do you mean?"

It didn't matter. I was tired of worrying. "I can't keep coming to you guys every time I need something."

"Sweetheart, we're your dads. That will never change."

"Speaking of relationships, Mrs. Goode left me a video. She said she was my grandmother."

They shifted in their seats, their sudden discomfort stunning.

"Wait, did you guys know?"

Papi bit down, his chiseled jaw working hard. "Yes, honey. We did."

My lungs froze for a solid thirty seconds. I recovered and asked, "For how long?"

"For a while now," Dad said in his soft Latino accent. "We made a promise—"

"You, too? That's what she said in the video."

"Cariña, have you watched the whole thing? It will explain—"

"You even knew about the video? Did you know about the house before I got the call?"

Another glance at each other told me everything I needed to know. "We knew your grandmother had planned on leaving it to you."

"Did you . . . did you know her?"

"Honey, watch the rest of the video."

I wanted to feel betrayed. I wanted to feel hurt and bitter and outraged. I failed. I loved these men so much. I trusted them implicitly. They would never do anything to hurt me. Not on purpose anyway.

"Get some rest, honey. Then finish the video. We'll call again in the morning."

"We love you," Papi said, flashing his killer smile.

"I love you, too."

We ended the call, and I sat in a state of absolute astonishment. They'd known. Questions came at me like bottle rockets, one after another. At least I knew for certain now.

A part of me thought Ruthie had the wrong person. It could happen. A mix-up with the adoption papers. A similar name and date-of-birth. But my dads knew her. It had to be legit, and that fact scared me a lot more than it should have.

I looked around. The house was just so beautiful, so dark and haunting and grim, my heart ached for Percy to be mine. I closed my laptop and put the papers aside. Then I lay back onto a down pillow, my hands clasped behind my head as I studied the ceiling. Ink snuggled beside me, his purr soothing. My lids grew heavy and I closed them.

"I can weigh my options with my eyes closed," I said to Ink. "Just for a minute." No sooner had I lowered my lids than another knock sounded at the door.

I startled awake, realizing I must have drifted off after all. The clock on my phone showed just past seven. I'd slept for almost four hours.

Ink had disappeared and was hopefully hunting for mice. Surely this place had mice.

Then I realized why I'd been awakened. Someone was pounding on my front door. Hard. What the hell? They'd just have to wait because my bladder would not.

Groggy and disoriented, I stumbled to the bathroom only to find a man on the floor. I skidded to a halt and looked down. Roane lay underneath the sink, visible only from the chest down. But, my God, what a lovely chest it was. And biceps. And calves. If only the kilt would slip up just a touch.

"Finished?"

I jumped so hard a little pee slipped out. Damn it.

He looked up at me from the ground, a wrench in his hands.

"Sorry. I was just admiring your kilt."

"Ah. Do you need the bathroom?"

"I can find another one. There's like thirty-two in this house."

One corner of his mouth rose. "Seven, actually."

"Plenty, then. You're here late."

His brows slid together, before saying, "Lots to do."

Understatement of the eon. "I can't believe this house has the original toilets." The tanks were wooden and hung from the walls with a pull rope to flush. I'd never seen one in real life. Now I'd get to see seven.

"Getting parts will be difficult, but I know a guy."

"I love that you know a guy because I don't. I wouldn't even know where to begin to find a guy to know and I'm going to search out a bathroom before I embarrass myself."

"Here," he said with a soft chuckle. He rolled onto his feet. "I need to get some parts anyway."

"Oh, can I use the sink?"

"Sure." He studied me for a few seconds, then added, "I've fixed it temporarily."

I stared back before coming to my senses. "Great. Thanks." He stepped around me to leave. "Oh, have you seen Ink?"

"Not since he came downstairs with an entire slice of pizza hanging from his mouth."

Oops. "Yeah, he was hungry."

"He's always hungry."

He left and it wasn't until that exact moment I realized something a little disturbing. To get to this bathroom, he had to come into Ruthie's room. My room. The one I'd been sleeping in.

I turned in a circle then spotted a cabinet that sat crooked against the wall.

I stepped to it and pulled. It swung wide, the opening leading to a finished passageway. A narrow hall that was softly lit by incandescent lighting.

"No way," I whispered to myself. A secret passageway. This was officially the coolest house I'd ever been in. And it could be mine for the low, low cost of every cent I made in the future for upkeep and restoration.

I couldn't decide if I was happier about the fact that

Percy had secret passageways or that Roane wasn't a creeper. It could go either way.

The knock sounded again. I closed the . . . cabinet, made quick work of the call from nature, washed my hands and dried them on a small towel as I headed down the stairs. About the time I got to the door, I realized I hadn't even glanced in the mirror.

That was okay. Whoever was knocking was clearly a pain in the ass.

The knock sounded again just as I turned the knob.

"Yes?" I said, letting my irritation show.

A man about my height with caramel hair and square plastic-framed glasses stood on the other side. "You must be Ms. Dayne."

"I must be." Amazing how many people knew my name here.

"I'm Donald. Donald Shoemaker. I live down the block." He pointed because that would help. "I'm here representing the North Shore Home Owners Association and the Beautify Salem Society. We just want you to know that we will no longer tolerate it. Any of it."

"I don't blame you."

"Ms. Dayne, if you don't take this seriously, we will be filing a lawsuit this afternoon."

Damn. I hadn't even been here a day and I already had a lawsuit against me? That beat my personal record, but just barely.

THREE

MEN: *Women are very hard to read.*
    WOMEN: *Actually, we just want—*
    MEN: *Such complex creatures.*
    WOMEN: *If you'd just liste—*
    MEN: *So mysterious.*
    -Actual Conversation

"Ms. Dayne, we've been trying to get Ruthie to do something about the situation for years."

I could tell Mr. Donald Shoemaker was going to be an issue for whomever ended up living here. Sadly, it would probably not be me, because I loved few things more than dressing down the Taylor Dooses of the world.

"She's repeatedly refused our requests. She even ignored our registered letters."

"She didn't." I wondered if I should tell Donald about the coffee stain on his starched baby-blue button-down.

"We at the NSHOA and BSS are certain you'll be more levelheaded."

"I wouldn't get my hopes up." Was it wrong that Donald reminded me of George McFly?

"This kind of thing is fine for the tourists in town. Not in this neighborhood. It's nice. Our properties are pristine, while this—" he paused to give Percy a once-over "—monstrosity gets drearier every year."

"You don't say."

The house trembled beneath our feet and I froze. It was slight, almost imperceptible, yet definitely there. After a minute, I asked Don, "Was that an earthquake?"

He took a wary step back and I couldn't believe I was going to do this dance again. We didn't even have music. I wondered if he would speed walk away like Mrs. Richter's assistant had.

Despite the spike of fear in his expression, he straightened his shoulders and set his jaw.

Attaboy.

"I'm here to see what you plan to do about it."

Speaking of tourists, I definitely needed to check out the town before I left. Surely walking around wouldn't cost me anything.

When I didn't answer, he added, "Ms. Dayne? Do you even have a plan?"

I snapped to attention. Or, well, pretended to. "Oh, sorry. What was the question?"

He spoke through gritted teeth. "What do you plan to do about the house now that it's yours?"

"Right. Well, first, I'm going to a supply store to buy a

no trespassing sign." I slammed the door and was headed for the stairs when he knocked again. Seriously, the *cojones*.

I swung the door open again, my face surely in flames.

"Can you please sign for this letter explaining what the NSHOA and BSS would like to see done?"

I was about to tell him which cavity he could insert his letter into when a feminine voice drifted to over us. "Oh, for the love of God, Donald. Get off that woman's porch."

We turned to see a fit middle-aged woman in a running suit walk up to the iron fence that surrounded the property.

"You stay out of this, Parris!" he shouted back.

That was apparently her cue. She walked through the gate and stomped toward us. "You'll have to forgive Donald. He had a difficult childhood."

Apparently having lost the battle, Donald tossed the letter onto Percy's porch and left in a literal huff.

I grinned at the woman. "I'm Defiance."

She took my hand. "That's a beautiful name."

"Thank you. Do you live—?"

"Right next door." She pointed to the house on Percy's north side. The white one with more splendor than Buckingham Palace. "I'm Parris. And that man," she said, pointing to a brunette working in the yard of the house on Percy's south side, "is my husband, Harris. So, let's just get that out of the way. Yes, we are Parris and Harris Hampton. If you ever need anything, we are literally next door."

"Thank you. Who lives in that house?" I gestured to the house where her husband was working. The one with grass so green and perfectly trimmed it looked like carpet. "And who does yardwork at this hour?"

"He does. On both counts."

"Your husband? Oh, I thought you said you lived—"

"I do. I live on your north and Harris lives on your south."

"Wow. That's unusual." Both houses were mansions, and I wondered what these people did for a living. "You live in separate houses?"

"Sure do. Which is why we're both still alive." She leaned in and touched my arm. "I love the man. Really I do. But I'd kill him if I had to live with him again. We figured separate living quarters would be easier to explain to the kids than why one of us had to go to prison for homicide."

Harris had walked around the fence and come inside the gate as well. He stepped onto the porch, both his tan and his hairline completely fake. "I'm Harris," he said, holding out his hand.

I took it. "Nice to meet you."

He had an easy grin and warm eyes. His wife's were more . . . calculating.

"Your grandmother was something else," he said. "I'm sorry for your loss."

How much personal info did one give complete strangers? And if I gave an inch, would they want to know the whole mile? Something told me the answer to that was *yes.* So I lied. "Thank you. I'm going to miss her."

"I'm sure." He gestured toward Percy. "I guess he's yours now."

I almost told them I couldn't keep Percy. For some reason, I changed my mind. They'd find out soon enough. "I guess. He's a lot to take in."

"He is," Parris said, taking Percy in, too.

I bent to pick up the letter Don had thrown down and wondered if I'd just picked up the proverbial gauntlet. "I don't think Donald likes him."

She laughed. "That's okay. Percival doesn't like Donald either."

Did everyone know about Percival's dark side? His seedy past?

A car pulled up to the gate. A taxi. After its brakes squealed it to a stop, a vertically challenged woman with a mop of curly, chestnut hair and turquoise cat-eye glasses got out.

"Annette?" My bestie wasn't supposed to arrive until tomorrow morning, yet here she was in all her windswept glory.

I hurried to greet her as the driver handed her an overnight bag, a carry-on, a suitcase, two grocery bags and a huge box. How long was she planning to stay?

"Nette the Jet."

She turned and beamed at me. "D-Bomb!"

I had no choice. I had to pull her into a hug, mostly because I knew she'd hate it.

"Yeah, still not a hugger," she said from the crook of my shoulder, fake-patting my back.

A giggle slipped past before I let her push off me and hold me at arm's length. She did it to get a good look at me. To assess the situation, as it were. Then her gaze drifted to the couple lip-locked behind me.

"Hosting orgies already?"

"Oh," I said, coming to my senses, "this is Parris and Harris Hampton. The neighbors."

They unlocked.

"Nice to meet you, Annette," Parris said. "We'll be going. Let you two catch up."

"Remember," Harris said, "we are right next door either way you turn." He chuckled at his own joke.

"Nice to meet you," I said to them, before turning back

to Annette. The love of my life. She was busy watching them walk in two separate directions when I snapped. "Wait, I thought you couldn't come until tomorrow. Why didn't you call me? I was going to pick you up from the airport."

She returned her attention to me and blinked. "I don't get it."

"You don't get what?"

"It is tomorrow." She looked at her watch. "It's 7:30 in the tomorrow morning."

"The tomorrow morning?" I screeched. I looked at my watch, too, before remembering I didn't wear one. "You mean, I slept all afternoon and all night?"

"'Parently. That can't be a good sign." She leaned in to study my pupils through her turquoise cat-eyes. "I wouldn't plan too far ahead. I see chaos. Turmoil. A fight with a tree branch that leads to your untimely and violent death."

Annette was a self-proclaimed expert in all things supernatural and supposedly psychic. The only thing she'd predicted accurately was the Superbowl of 2013. I never pointed out the fact that she'd had a 50/50 chance.

"Good to know."

Last week I was supposed to die from a tragic fall while trying to stand up in a hammock. Who would even do that?

"Dephne," she said as she picked up the carry-on and dragged her massive suitcase past me, her voice filled with awe. "You have to keep this place. Two words. B and B."

I picked up the box and followed. "Those are letters, and it would take a crap-ton of money to turn this into a B and B. Money that I don't have."

"Better yet, a boutique hotel. Witch themed. We can hold séances!" She tried to jump up and down in excitement, but her load proved a hindrance. She dropped it inside the foyer then turned a full circle in awe.

I set down the box. "Séances? I guess now's the time I should remind you that you aren't actually psychic."

She stopped and glared at me. "My powers are emerging. It takes time."

"You've been trying to contact the dead since we were in high school."

"And what makes you think I haven't succeeded?"

"The fact that you haven't?"

"Mark my words, I will become one of the most powerful witches—"

"Now you're a witch?"

She beamed at me then whirled to examine more of what Percy had to offer. "I am if we're staying in Salem."

"We?" Excitement prickled along my skin. "Nette, are you saying you'd come with me? You'd move here?"

She turned to me, her expression full of warmth. "In a heartbeat. It's the only way I can get back that fifty bucks you owe me."

My expression flatlined. "Of course it is."

"Now, where's kilt guy and what in the blistering hell is that?"

I followed her gaze to Ink. He was sneaking down the stairs, dragging yet another slice of pizza beside him. "That is a cat. His name is Ink and he likes me, so be nice."

"It doesn't look like a cat."

"It is."

"It looks like a mangled ferret."

"It isn't."

"Can it be a cat somewhere else?"

"No."

"And the guy?"

"He's upstairs."

She put her purse on a wing-back, and asked, "Verdict?"

"Okay, you know those scruffy men on calendars with messy shoulder-length hair and insane tat-covered muscles?"

"Like the back of my hand."

"He's that."

"Dayum."

"And he knows a lot more than most about my vagina."

"Way to go, you!"

I shrugged. My phone beeped and I saw the thirty messages from Annette wondering where I was and why I wasn't at the airport and did I understand how much a taxi was going to cost, so, my bad.

She began gathering up her things again.

"What is all of this?"

"What? I told you I didn't travel light."

"Sorry about the taxi."

"Please. You clearly needed the sleep."

My phone beeped again with a notification from Etsy, and the clouds parted to let the sun shine down on me in particular.

"Oh, my God. I sold three journals last night! I can afford a sandwich! Let's go to lunch!"

"It's 7:30 in the morning."

"Let's go to breakfast!"

———

ROANE HAD DISAPPEARED AGAIN, so we took turns showering while Ink looked on in mild fascination. Or utter annoyance. It was hard to tell.

"This one-bathroom thing is fun and all," she said, "but don't you have, like, thirty?"

"I have seven. I need to stock the others. Roane is checking out all the plumbing."

She snickered. "I bet he is."

We took the bug to a hotel pub by the water called The Regatta. Beautifully decorated with dark woods and blue accents, the pub was clearly a favorite with the locals.

"Welcome to Witch City," our adorable server said when she found out we weren't from the area. She put down our drinks and left to put in our order.

"Witch City," Annette said. "How cool is that?"

I felt the history of the town to the marrow of my bones. Salem was rich and eclectic and full of darkness and light. Of good and evil. Of pain and sorrow. And a joy born of survival after a time when hysteria reigned.

The people had sojourned past the tragic events that made them famous and built a life for themselves. Now, almost 300 years later, their descendants reaped the benefits.

Annette looked up from her travel guide, which could have been how our server knew we weren't locals. "Did you know there's an alley here in Salem that you walk down and, if you know the secret password, you get free bacon?"

"Where'd you get that book?" I asked, a little jealous.

"A bookstore in the airport. It's over there somewhere." She pointed in the general direction of Massachusetts.

"I can't keep the house," I blurted, because blurting bad news was kind of my specialty. Otherwise, I lived in a constant state of denial. A sadness washed over me with the confession. "I just don't have the money."

"What about the restaurant? It's doing well, right?"

I'd owned a restaurant in Phoenix called The Papidad,

after my dads. Like everything else I'd owned, I lost it in the divorce.

"It's doing great as far as I know."

Annette stilled. "Wait, you're kidding me. He got it?"

"More like his mother got it, with his help."

"Deph, how is that even possible?"

"It was in her name, remember? We needed her to co-sign to get us started. What I didn't know is that Kyle put everything in her name. The restaurant. The house. The cars. Even the bank accounts. When it came time to split everything, I basically had nothing to split. Now he has it all."

"A good lawyer—"

"Would have cost me a fortune."

Her face started to blotch, which meant her insides were way angrier than her outsides were letting on. It was also why she sucked at poker. "How could you keep this from me?"

"I didn't want you to know how incredibly naïve I am."

"Not naïve. Just far too trusting."

"Isn't that the definition of naïve?"

"If I were a hugger, I'd be on you like green on guacamole right now."

That was staying a lot. "Thanks, Nette. It's the thought that counts."

"That's exactly what I told my credit card company when my payment was late. What do your dads think? And have either of them decided to go straight? Because damn."

I laughed. "No. Sorry. The minute they do, you'll be the first to know."

"What do they think about all of this."

"It's my mess, Nette. I didn't want to bring them into it."

"So, you let that asshat and his bitch mother take everything from you instead? You built that place from the ground up. You created specialized menus for different dietary needs. You crafted culinary masterpieces other restaurants could only dream of making. You put nine dimes out of ten back into it. And now it's all theirs?"

"Every last inch."

I could tell the conversation was raising her blood pressure, which was exactly why I hadn't told her all the sordid details. Well, that and pride.

"Sweetheart, how broke are you?"

"Preface the word *broke* with the word *dead* and you'll nail it."

The blotchiness disappeared and a bright blush blossomed across her face. It was born of an anger that ran deep in that girl. Deep deep. So, so deep. Like Nietzsche dee—

"I can't believe you didn't tell your dads."

I released a long sigh of defeat. "What could they have done?"

"Killed your ex and buried his lifeless body in the Sonoran. Duh." The mere thought put a dreamy smile on her face.

"What would I do without you?"

"I can think of lots of things. Go skydiving. Try escargot. Belly dance, because not in my wildest dreams."

A male voice interrupted her rant. "Excuse me."

We looked up in unison, and I watched through my periphery as Annette melted like ice cream on a sidewalk in August. A tall, uniformed officer stood beside our table. Wide-shouldered and hazel-eyed, he had dark skin and a kind face and I melted a little, too.

"Hey, Chief," someone called out to him.

He nodded then turned back to us. "You must be Defiance," he said to me.

What the hell? Did everyone know me?

"I am." I shook his hand. "This is Annette."

When he offered her his hand, she took his one into both of hers, her expression turning grave, her gaze sliding past him so she could see beyond the veil into another realm.

And we were off.

"I'm Houston Metcalf. Most people just call me Chief, but please call me Houston."

"Your aura," Annette said from the beyond. "You're kind and fair. A good officer of the law. Yet I fear you will lose yourself if you don't find true love. Now. Like this very minute."

The grin that spread across his face told me he was not only used to such airheaded declarations, but he was not buying her aura schtick for a minute. Smart guy.

He took back his hand. "Thank you, ma'am. I'll keep an eye out." He winked at me. "Your grandmother told me you were coming. I'm glad I spotted you."

"And how did you do that, exactly?"

"Arizona tags."

"Right. Those give me away every time. But how did you know who I was? Like, here in the restaurant?"

He suddenly looked uncomfortable and straightened his belt. "Buddy in Phoenix PD. He forwarded me the photo from your license."

"You could've just looked on Facebook" Annette offered super helpfully.

He let out a deep laugh. "There is that." He turned back to me. "Your grandmother said you were a beauty."

While I wanted to ask, how? How did she know? Why didn't she come find me? I asked instead, "You knew her?"

His mouth thinned and a sadness came over him. "I did. I'm sorry for your loss."

That statement, a statement that had seemed so foreign to me one day ago, was now very much appreciated. It *was* a loss. I would never get the chance to know the incomparable Ruthie Goode. People seemed to either love her or hate her. No in between. No willy-nilly. I got the feeling she didn't hold back much.

"Thank you."

"Well, I'll let you finish your breakfast. I just wanted to introduce myself. Let you know if there's anything you need, I'm only a phone call away." He handed me his card. "Just not through 9-1-1. Ruthie loved to call me through 9-1-1."

A soft laugh covered up my awe of the woman. "I appreciate it."

He started to walk off, but he turned back. "And, in case you're wondering, we're hoping you stay."

"We?" I asked, more than a little surprised.

"The town." He spread his arms, indicating the patrons of the restaurant, and each and every one of them was looking at me. It stunned me for a moment. I was not a fan of attention. Then a few raised their glasses in welcome.

I'd never seen anything like it nor felt so welcome. "Thank you," I said, before ducking my head as a soft heat infused my cheeks.

"See?" Annette clinked her coffee cup against mine. "Even Witch City wants you to stay."

The very thought filled me with a strange, unfamiliar joy. I knew a ton of people in Phoenix, but I would never have received such a reception. Not that anyone would. Maybe the president. No. Not even him. The pope?

A thought popped into my head and I refocused on my compadre. "I forgot to tell you the best part about Percival."

"I like all his parts already. This must be good."

Leaning in, I pasted a wicked grin on my face, and said, "Two words. Secret passageway."

Her hand slowly made its way across the table. It covered mine, and she said softly, "Holy mother of God."

FOUR

I'm a coffeeholic on the road to recovery.
Just kidding.
I'm on the road to the coffee shop.
-True Story

"This kilt guy. He has a key to the house?" Annette asked when we got back to Percy and tossed our bags on the sheet-covered wingback.

"Apparently. And before you say anything, Ruthie trusted him enough—"

"Oh, no, I don't care about that. I'm just wondering when I get mine."

"Of course, you are."

I had to show her the entrance to the secret passageway, at least the one I knew about, and pinky-swear we'd explore passages later. But I only had two more days to decide if I was going to even attempt to keep the house. I needed to take a closer look at the finances.

Nette hadn't been wrong. This place would make an amazing B&B. Or, like she said, an incredible boutique hotel. Maybe if I got a job. A job that paid $25,000 per hour. I had a bachelor's, but because nothing felt right and I couldn't decide what I wanted to do with my life, I got the degree in liberal arts. I couldn't come up with a single job in my area of expertise that would pay me what I needed to make a dent in this place.

There was simply no way I could afford to keep it. Not without involving my dads, and that was not going to happen. I'd put them through enough.

I knew my failed marriage and subsequent state of empty pocket syndrome weighed on them, no matter how much they tried to hide it. They'd both aged over the last few months. Dad was in his late sixties already. He didn't need me shoving him closer to the pearly gates.

We went back downstairs for coffee and to hopefully run into a certain journeyman. Instead we found a scruffy cat complaining about his water bowl being empty.

I put on a pot seconds before Annette put her hands on my shoulders and turned me to face her, a look of sheer determination in her eyes. "Defiance."

"Annette," I shot back, suddenly wary.

"I think it's time I meet your grandmother. Anyone who decorated with this kind of underworld panache needs to be worshipped, and worship her I shall."

I bit my bottom lip. "The video?"

She nodded. "The video."

My plan had been to finish watching Ruthie's message last night. Alone. So I could melt down in peace if I needed to. I could still melt down with Annette by my side, it would just be embarrassing. At least Ink wouldn't have heckled me.

We sat down at the breakfast table with our cups and I opened up the file.

"What are these other files in the folder?"

"I'm not sure yet. I just clicked on the one titled Defiance."

The lovely Ruthie Goode came into view again, frozen where I'd paused yesterday, her blond, shoulder-length bob cut to inspire elegance and style. The moment I went to click on play, a knock sounded at the back door not ten feet from us.

I walked over and opened it. A young woman stood on the back porch, bouncing from one foot to the other, her expression panicked. She had gorgeous tawny skin, a light sprinkling of freckles and huge, expressive eyes. Her black curly hair had been pulled back into a ponytail and her jacket sat askew and inside out on her shoulders.

The strangest thing about her visit, however, was that she'd come to the back door. I wondered if she knew Ruthie well. If she knew she'd passed.

I'd barely gotten out a "Hi" before she barged past me, her gaze flitting about wildly.

"I'm so sorry to bother you. You're Defiance, right?"

Again with this?

"I'm Dana. Dana Hart. I'm across the way, a couple houses down over on Warren. I'm so sorry about Ruthie. I can't imagine what you're going through, but I lost my ring." She stopped and eyed me, clearly wanting a response. "My wedding ring."

I glanced at Annette whose only contribution was a shrug.

Dana was nearly hyperventilating, so I offered her a chair.

"Oh, no, I couldn't possibly," she said, sinking into the seat.

I sat beside her and took her hand in mine to help calm her.

"I can't believe it. It was on the sink and then it wasn't. I've torn my house apart. I've taken off that catch thing underneath the sink? You know, where the water flows? Nothing. I've even combed through my dog's poop. Nothing. Absolutely nothing."

After retrieving my hand from hers, I glanced at Annette again. She was much more helpful this time. She made the crazy gesture, winding her index finger around her ear. Discreetly, though. So Dana wouldn't see.

"It's nowhere." She slammed me with a look of such utter desperation, my heart went out to her. It broke free from my rib cage and flew on angel wings to this strange, hysterical person.

Then I felt it again. That quake beneath my feet.

Dana had felt it, too. She paused long enough to look up and say, "I'm sorry. I'm just so upset. I didn't mean to ignore you, Percy. How are you?" Without waiting for an answer— which could take a while—she bolted out of the chair and went back to pacing. "You have to find it for me. Whittington's coming back tomorrow night. It was his great, great, great, great grandmother's, or some crap, passed down from Hart woman to Hart woman for generations, and I'm the one who loses it. The family will never forgive me."

"Dana," I said, risking my life by stepping into her path. But I had to. She was wearing a trench in my floor.

She stopped, her gaze landing on me at last.

"Will you sit down so we can talk about this? I'm not sure how I'm supposed to help you find your ring, but . . ."

Her lashes blinked in such rapid succession, I feared

they would take flight. "I don't understand." She glanced at Annette then back at me. "You're Defiance, right?"

"Yes. Would you like to sit—?"

"Ruthie's granddaughter?"

"So I've been told."

"Then . . . I don't get it."

I gave up and sat down myself. "Dana, why would you think I can help you find your wedding ring?"

The snort that escaped from her lovely mouth was almost as humorous as the perplexed look on Annette's face. "Because you're Ruthie's granddaughter."

"Okay."

"You . . . are . . . Ruthie's . . . granddaughter," she repeated, slower this time, enunciating each syllable.

This was getting us absolutely nowhere. "Please, sit down."

She finally lowered herself into the chair next to me, now as wary of me as I was of her.

"What does my being Ruthie's granddaughter have to do with you finding your ring?"

A bout of nervous laughter bubbled out of her. She sobered, and repeated, "I don't get it."

"Yes, you said that."

"No, I mean, you're Defiance Dayne. Ruthie told me all about your—Oh, my God!" Her hands flew to her mouth. "You don't want people to know. You want to be incognito. Like Batman. Or Superman. Or Ted Bundy. You want your identity to remain a secret."

What in the love of crystal meth was this woman on? She'd looked so normal. I'd heard heroin was big again, especially with desperate housewives.

"I am so sorry," she continued. "I haven't told anyone. I swear. I'm probably the only person in town who knows about you. Well, one of maybe three." She looked up and counted on her fingers. "Four tops."

Okay, enough of this. I took her hands and pulled her to her feet. "Dana, we have a lot of work to do. Maybe we can come over later and help you look? How does that sound?"

"No!" She dug in her heels. "You have to help me. His family will never forgive me."

"How am I supposed to help you?" I asked, exasperated.

"With . . . you know." She lifted her shoulders and made a face like we were sharing some deep, dark secret.

"You're right," I said, urging her toward the door again. "I'll look into it. Swear."

Just when I'd gotten her halfway out the door, she gasped and whirled around again. "Wait. You *don't* know."

"Know what?" Annette asked, chiming in at last.

She ignored her and kept her gaze locked onto me like I'd just grown another head. "How can you not know?"

"Thanks for stopping by," I said, shooing her out the door. She'd gone from frantic to bewildered to dumb-founded in a matter of minutes.

"You have to help me."

"We will. We'll stop by later. How's that?" I didn't wait for an answer. I shut the door.

She stood there staring at me through the glass like a lost puppy dog.

"God, I love this town," Annette said.

"Yeah. Sure. Me, too." Even though I said the words, I was beginning to wonder about it.

After reheating my coffee, I sat down again. Annette kept her gaze locked onto me, watching my every move.

"What?" I asked.

"Nothing. That was just weird."

"Yes, it was. Where are your psychic abilities when I need them? You could've warned me about her."

"I think they're on the fritz. I think Percy is blocking them."

I woke up my laptop and Annette scooted closer for a better view. "She was so lovely, your grandmother."

"Wasn't she?" I clicked play.

Ruthie started speaking immediately. "We don't have a lot of time, honey. If you're watching this, I've passed over, and you need to protect yourself. I know I've thrown a lot at you. I wish I could've found you and explained everything in person, but we have to get past that, now. Your life depends on it."

Annette hit pause. "We need to be writing this stuff down. It'll make a great movie of the week someday. It's all so theatrical."

I took a sip, then asked, "Why would my life depend on anything?"

"No clue, but it does suck to be you at the moment." She hit play again.

"I know that sounds a bit theatrical," Ruthie continued. "Like a movie of the week."

"Oh, my God." Annette hit pause again and touched her fingertips to her parted lips. "I really am psychic."

Oh, for the love of puppies. I hit play.

"Please trust me. Just for a little while. Just until I know you're safe."

She waited, then, as though expecting me to answer.

"I need you to do something, and then I will explain in vivid detail why. I just need you to do this one thing first. Deal?"

"Deal," I said aloud. To no absolutely one.

"Okay. I need you to—"

A knock sounded again. This time from the front door. I pressed pause. "What now?"

Annette shrugged again, even though she was busy frowning at Ruthie's image, her mind working overtime. "Did you see that?"

"I'll be right back."

I answered the door to a twenty-something male, slim with sandy hair. He had a very familiar expression on his face, the same one as my last visitor.

"Hi, are you Mrs. Goode's granddaughter?"

"Apparently," I said for the umpteenth time. "What can I do for you?"

He stepped closer, pleading.

My hand tightened around the doorknob I clung to. I wasn't about to let this one inside.

"My girlfriend is missing. She's been missing for over a week now. I need you to find her."

I realized Annette had walked up behind me.

"Look," I said, getting aggravated. "I don't know where you're getting your information—"

"Please." He twisted a baseball cap in his fists. "The cops haven't turned up anything. Their investigation has stalled. I need someone who can actually do some good."

"Mr. . . .?

"Scott. Wade Scott. I have money. Not much. I can get more, though. Anything. Just name your price."

As much as that thought perked up my broke little ears, I shook my head at him, confused. "Mr. Scott, I don't know what you expect me to do."

His face morphed from frantic to confusion, much like Dana's had. "You're Mrs. Goode's granddaughter, right? You're related?"

This was getting ridiculous. "Look, I'm so sorry for what you're going through. Really, I am, but I can't help you."

"I don't understand."

"You and me both."

I went to close the door, but he held up a hand. "Wait." He fished a card out of his shirt pocket. "If you change your mind." He handed it to me. It was a business card for a Scott Construction. "And this." He handed me a picture, supposedly of his girlfriend, a pretty brunette. "That's Sara. If you change your mind." He stepped even closer. "Please change your mind."

The muscles in my chest tightened as I slid the door closed.

"Seriously, Deph," Annette said. "What on God's green?"

"What on God's green indeed." We headed back to the table. "How can I help anyone find anything? And what does my likely relation to Ruthie have to do with it?"

Annette stopped as a thought occurred to her. "Dude, she was a PI. She had to be. That's the only explanation."

"Maybe."

She poured us some more coffee. "It has to be. And for some reason everyone thinks you're going into the same business." She handed my cup back.

"Thank you. So, is it going to be like this all the time? I don't think I can handle many more of these visits."

"Surely not. I mean, once people figure out you have no talent whatsoever, especially when it comes to investigations, they'll stop bugging you. I'm certain of it." She patted my back for reassurance.

"I guess. Thanks, Nette. You're the best."

"Don't mention it."

Before we could hit play again, another knock sounded on the front door.

I gaped at my bestie. She gaped back, before casting another quizzical expression at the screen of my laptop.

"That's it. I'll take care of this."

"Atta girl," she said.

I marched to the door and opened it to an insanely tall man with a tweed jacket and pencil mustache.

"No," I said, then started to close the door.

"Ms. Dayne?" he said, hesitant.

I stopped and gave him my best expression of sympathy. "I get it. You've lost something. Or someone. But I'm full up. I can't help you."

"Ms. Dayne, wait. I'm from Santander Bank."

"A bank? Don't tell me. You got robbed, right?"

"Well—"

"And you need someone to find the money? Or maybe the thief. Either way, I am not your girl. I have zero investigative skills no matter how talented my grandmother apparently was, so you're wasting your time. Pinky swear."

"I just need a moment—"

"Sorry. Not today." I felt bad, but it had to be done. I slammed the door in his face. Poor guy.

I turned and ran smack dab into a brick wall. A brick wall covered in muscle and ink.

"Roane," I said, stepping back. "Sorry. I didn't mean to mow you over."

He lifted an amused brow.

"Well, you know, run into you."

He wore a different tee, a black one that brought out the color in his tattoos, but he wore that same kilt. Then again, maybe he had a whole collection. A girl could dream. This time, he had a round hunk of metal in his hands. The way he held it in his long, strong fingers—careful yet firm, rather like the way I wished he would hold my ass—sent a shot of yearning straight to my abdomen. My abdomen hadn't yearned in a long time.

"I'm going out for a sprocket," he said. "I'll be back in twenty."

Clearing my throat, I recovered. Feigned coolness. "Oh, good. We can always use more sprockets."

That lazy grin made another appearance. "What did Mr. Bourne want?"

"Mr. Bourne?"

He gestured toward the door. "The banker."

"Oh." I waved a dismissive hand. "Who knows? People keep knocking on my door wanting me to find things for them. I can barely find my sanity when I need it. Why would they think I could find their things?"

The look he graced me with, one of curiosity and, if I didn't know better, admiration, sent an electrical shockwave from the top of my head to the tips of my toes. "I don't know," he said, dropping his gaze to the metal object in his hands, "you found me."

For a long moment, I forgot how to breathe. He was so sincere. And almost, for a split second, vulnerable. I refocused and decided to tease him. "Yeah, well, you were standing in my kitchen half-naked. It was hard *not* to find you."

I stood there basking in the glow of his olive eyes. They shimmered even in the low light. I stared too long. He stared back. The moment should have been awkward. It was anything but.

He recovered first. "Do you need anything while I'm out?"

"No, but Ink might want more pizza. He took the last slice."

He laughed softly. "Sorry about that."

"Not at all. He's adorable in a demolition derby kind of way."

"That's Ink," he said with a nod before heading out the door. I watched as long as I could, fighting the urge to ask him if I could have his babies, then I hightailed it back to the kitchen.

"A banker," I said to Annette when I walked back in. "And Roane went out to get sprockets."

"I missed him again?" she asked, her gaze glued to the screen.

"It's your turn to answer the door. Just tell them I've slipped into a coma and the prognosis is grim and what in the blazing saddles are you doing?"

She was staring at the screen, her face the picture of concentration. "Just watch."

I joined her and we stared at Ruthie Goode for a solid two minutes before I asked, "What are we looking for? She's on pause."

"Exactly. Just wait."

"No." At the rate we were going, I'd never finish the video, and it was only thirteen minutes and thirteen seconds long. Which was odd. I pressed play and Ruthie began talking again.

"I know you're going to wonder why, but I need you to draw a symbol in the air while thinking about protection." She lifted a drawing. It reminded me of a treble clef, two loops on top of each other with a wavy line down the center. "Can you draw this in the air for me with your hand? And remember, concentrate on the idea of protection."

"This is getting so weird," Annette said, her tone full of anticipation.

I crossed my arms. "Is this a test? Like for physical dexterity or something?"

Ruthie showed her palms. "I know this sounds strange, sweetheart. Please just trust me. Please do this. I'll wait."

I let out a loud breath. Annette watched as I raised a hand and tried to draw the symbol.

"Start here," Ruthie added, pointing to the bottom of the first loop. "With two fingers, maybe. I'm not really sure. I'm not like you. But start here, loop one, loop two, then wave down."

I paused the video. "I feel like an idiot." Turning to Annette, I realized she'd brought out her phone. "Don't you dare film this."

She snorted. "How can I not?"

I grabbed the phone, laid it on the table, and tried again.

"No, no, no. Not like that, honey," Ruthie said. "I think you have to start at the bottom."

Annette and I both snapped back to the screen, our jaws coming unhinged.

"I thought I put that on pause."

"I knew it," Annette said.

I gaped at her. "You knew what?"

Ruthie was now waiting, supposedly for me to complete the task. She chewed on her lower lip and looked to the side as if to avoid eye contact.

Annette leaned closer, squinting her eyes. "She heard the knock. Before. She'd stopped talking when that banker knocked, even before you hit pause."

I eased back, putting distance between me and the woman in the video. "That's not possible."

"And then, while you were talking to him, she blinked. I

saw it." She pointed at Ruthie, her tone accusing, like the woman had done something wrong.

Wait, she had done something wrong!

"Ruthie Goode," I said, my voice razor-sharp. "Are you still alive?"

"Have you drawn the symbol?" she asked, her voice hesitant.

"Are we on Skype or something?"

"It's very important that you draw it correctly or it won't work."

I leaned closer, my face inches from the screen, and said, "I will close this laptop right now if you don't tell me what's going on. Where are you?"

She deflated and looked back at us. "I'm sorry. I thought this would work."

I bolted back, knocking over the chair. "You're alive?"

A sadness lowered her shoulders even more. "No, honey. I died. Just like Mrs. Richter told you. But before I passed, I created a spell that would allow me to communicate with you, and this is the best I could do. You're in terrible danger."

"A spell?" Annette asked, fascinated.

"I'm a witch."

"Oh, my God." She covered her mouth with both fists to keep from squealing. "I've died and gone to heaven."

"Salem, actually." Ruthie winked at her. "Pretty darn close."

"Ruthie," I said, my tone soft, placating, "you aren't dead. You can't be. It doesn't work like that."

"You are so beautiful," she said, her eyes glistening. "I wanted to meet you so often. Instead, I had you watched. I received regular updates about you and your life and your friends."

"Watched? Like by a private investigator?"

"Something like that. I'll explain. I promise I will, but my death broke the protection spell I had on you."

"Ruthie, a lot of people think you've passed away. You can't do that to them."

"She did pass away," Annette said, falling for every word.

"Okay, let's pretend I'm still alive."

"You are," I said.

"Will you make the symbol? Just try."

"I will." I raised my chin. "When we meet face-to-face." Did she not want to meet me?

A cabinet door slammed beside us so hard, it shook the house. Annette screamed and jumped away, her lids like saucers from behind her cat-eye glasses.

Ruthie nodded in resignation. "Don't be mad, Percival. She doesn't understand yet."

I'd jumped at the sound, too, but now I stood frozen, my mind racing, trying to figure out what was going on. All the while, my body fought for control. It wanted me out of there. Out of the house. Out of Salem.

"I can see this isn't going to work until you know the truth. Until you believe the truth. Go to Houston. The police chief you met. He'll show you my body."

A sense of dread took root and snaked its way throughout my entire being. "Ruthie—"

"Go, sweetheart. Hurry. I'll be here when you get back. But please be careful."

FIVE

Sometimes someone unexpected comes
into your life and makes your heart race.
We call these people cops.
-Meme

Chief Metcalf had been expecting us. I didn't ask him how. He stood when we walked into his office at the police station. The officer who led us back offered us coffee, but I couldn't speak, so Annette politely declined. He closed the door behind us.

"Defiance," the chief said, gesturing to two chairs. "Annette. Nice to see you again."

"What's going on?" I asked, finding my voice at last.

"If you'll just sit down—"

"I'm good. Please, Chief Metcalf, what is going on?"

"Call me Houston." He was graying at the temples. It made him look even more distinguished.

"She's not dead."

"Yes, sweetheart, she is."

"She's—she's in the video."

"It was the only way. Something about the radio waves being compatible with the veil? I don't know all of the technical stuff."

"She's not dead." I felt like I was losing my grandmother all over again. And I'd just found her. "This stuff isn't real. It doesn't exist."

"Come on." He led us out the door. We got in his cruiser and he took us to the funeral home.

The dread began suffocating me. He spoke softly with the funeral director, a stark gentleman with a sharp, angular face and round glasses, then took us to a room where we waited in absolute silence. Even Annette had nothing to say, the weight of the home crushing.

After a few minutes, the director and an assistant wheeled out a coffin. As I looked at it, my vision blurred. I blinked back the stinging wetness.

"I'm paying for the funeral if you don't mind, Defiance."

The director looked at me in surprise. "Defiance Goode?"

Paying for the funeral had been the last thing on my mind, but I knew those things cost a fortune. What struck me most, however, was the fact that my name was originally Defiance Goode. It was so foreign and yet settled around me like an old blanket.

"Dayne," the chief corrected.

"You're Ruthie's granddaughter? I am so sorry for your loss," he said, his words seemingly genuine as he took my hand. "She was something else."

The assistant opened the coffin to reveal a stunning older woman who looked nowhere near the eighty years she had to be. Her blond hair had been dressed and a light dusting of makeup gave color to her pale skin.

"She was a looker," the chief said, and then the funeral thing finally sank in.

"Why are you paying for her funeral?"

"It's the least I can do. She . . . she helped me when I wasn't even aware I needed help."

Annette, whom I just realized had been holding my hand since we arrived, said to him, "You loved her."

He pressed his mouth together. "More than anything on this earth."

I looked at her again. Stepped closer. Brushed my fingertips across her porcelain face. "I just . . . this isn't real."

"She wanted one of those natural burials. You know the kind. No embalming fluid. Just her finding her way back to nature."

Even in death, she had an air about her. A genteel quality. "This isn't real," I repeated, my voice hitching.

"I'm so sorry," the chief said, before pulling me into a hug.

I hugged back.

"YOU HAD A TWIN, RIGHT?" I asked Ruthie when we got back to the house, my voice somber. "I had a great aunt?"

She'd had her back to . . . what? The camera? Surely they didn't have cameras on the other side, and I realized with that one thought I was totally buying into all of this.

She whirled around. "I'm sorry, sweetheart. I wanted to know you more than anything in the world."

"Then why? If you were having me watched, you knew where I was. You knew who'd adopted me. Why not come find me?" I felt like a child, wondering why her parents didn't love her. All those feelings of abandonment resurfaced in one, gut-wrenching blow.

Annette was making a pot of coffee while I threw my pity party. She glanced over her shoulder in apprehension.

"I can explain," Ruthie said.

"Please, do."

She filled her lungs. "I will. I swear. As soon as you—"

"Make the stupid symbol? How is this real, Ruthie? How is any of this real?"

"I told you. I'm a witch, but there's more to it than that. I—we—come from a long line of very powerful witches. We can do things mundane witches, those who come to the religion voluntarily, can't."

"Things like live forever thanks to Wi-Fi?"

"Well, no, this is new. It took me years and years of research to figure out how to do this. We can come back from the veil, yes. Communication is where it gets tricky. I needed a way to communicate with you. To explain who you are. Or, more importantly, what you are."

"Why wait then? Why not find me sooner and tell me all of this while you were still alive?"

"I made a promise."

"To who?" I asked, my voice rising an octave with frustration. "Who could you possibly promise something so inane—"

"You."

I stopped and sat back in my chair. "What?"

"I promised you, my darling girl. You are everything. I had to keep you safe."

"Why?"

"You're not like me. Not entirely. You are what is called a source. Or, in some circles, a charmling."

Annette sat down and slid a cup to me. I ignored it.

"You are the rarest breed of mystical creature in the known realm."

"What realm? What are you even talking about?"

"The known realm."

"What is the known realm?"

"I don't know. It's the realm that's known. The important thing is, you are a charmling, and as such, we don't have much time."

"What does that mean?"

"Sweetheart, we don't have time."

"What. Does. That. Mean?"

"Okay, then." She shrugged and sat down. I just couldn't tell on what. "Witch 101 it is. When a witch uses her powers, she has to draw energy from living things. Or, things that were once alive. Herbs, animals, insects."

"I've seen the movies."

"Oh, I have, too," Annette said, chiming in.

"But a source, a charmling, *is* energy. Pure, dynamic energy. You don't need to pull energy from an outside source to create magic because you generate your own. You are a walking, breathing, self-sustaining nuclear powerplant."

A dubious grin formed on my mouth, and I waved an index finger back and forth. "You almost had me."

"Oh, come on," Annette said. "This is gold."

"Gold covered BS is still BS. I am no different than any other person on the street. I think I would've known."

"Oh, you are, darling girl. Comparing the average person to you is like comparing a candle's flame to the sun. You are so much more powerful than you realize. But you can be killed. Especially now. We need to perform—"

"Okay, how did all of this come about? Why am I so different from you?"

"You were born a charmling."

"Then my dad was a charmling?"

"No, the power can only be held by a female."

"As it should be," Annette said.

"Then my mom?"

"No. That's why you were such a surprise, to say the least. To give you an idea of what I mean, your birth was comparable to the birth of an illegitimate child in a crack house only to find out that child is of royal blood and next in line to be the queen of England." She'd stopped, then added, "If an illegitimate child born in a crack house could hold the English throne, that is."

"Then if not my mom or dad—"

"I said your father wasn't a charmling himself. He couldn't have been. That means he had to have charmling blood flowing through his veins. Perhaps his mother was one. Or his grandmother. That's the only explanation." She shook her head, dismissing the quandary. "It doesn't matter. Since we don't know who he is, we have no way of knowing which family he's from. And, Defiance," she said, leaning closer, "that's not a good thing."

"Great," I said, the word dripping with sarcasm. "Let's say, for argument's sake, I buy this. How did any of it come about?"

"Sweetheart, we don't have time."

"Let's make the time." I folded my arms over my chest and she lifted her hands, acquiescing.

"Okay, Charm 101: An Introduction to All Things Charmling."

"Thank you."

"The charmlings were created by original witches thousands of years ago. They were a coven, and they saw the injustice women suffered at the hands of men, even in the witch realm. They sought to balance the power by creating three beings no man can defeat."

"I like it," Annette said.

"They pooled their power and the power of their ancestors and funneled it into three witches to be a beacon of light. A balance of power."

"There are only three of us? Charmlings?"

"Yes. When one charmling dies, either another witch inherits that power or, if a girl is born of charmling blood, that baby inherits it. The baby takes precedence always."

"Then why hide me away?"

"There are those who wouldn't hesitate to kill you to get your power. I had to hide you."

"And the other two charmlings? You know who they are?"

"Yes. They're very protected. They're celebrities in the witch world, even though most of us don't believe they were born of royal blood. They were simply witches until they were created by killing a true charmling and stealing her power. We believe you are the first true charmling born in over two hundred years."

"Great. This mad rush with the protection spell, is someone out to get me?"

She dropped her gaze. "Those dark forces are always on the lookout for the third charmling. Hunters were dispatched the moment you were born. They would kill you in a heartbeat, Defiance. But that's the thing. A charmling is the most powerful supernatural being on the planet. Once you establish your shield, once you protect yourself, you cannot be as easily killed."

"As easily? You mean they'd have to use a sledge-hammer or something?" It was bizarre to be talking about my impending doom so casually.

"Not even then," she said with a soft husky laugh. "I just wanted to keep you safe, so I hid your power. Diffused it, if you will. I made it so that no other creature, human or witch, could pinpoint your location. My spell is like a GPS blocker."

"But now that you're gone?"

"My spell is gone. You're vulnerable, and I guarantee there are forces in play as we speak, making plans to steal your power. We have to reactivate the shield, the GPS blocker. We have to diffuse your power so that even other witches think you are simply one of their own."

"Okay, let me get this straight. There are witches," I said, ignoring her pleas, "and there are charmlings. What else is out there, hidden in plain sight?"

"That's pretty much it. Oh, well, besides demons, though they hardly ever bother anyone. They have an undeservedly sullied reputation. What you have to under-stand is that charmlings *are* witches. Just very, very powerful ones."

"Wait a minute," Annette said, holding her hands in a time-out T. She turned to me, aghast. "You're a witch?"

I glanced at Ruthie then back. "'Parently."

"*You* . . . are a witch."

"That's the word on the street."

"A witch."

"Dude, you have to stop." This was getting embar-rassing.

"You," she repeated, the disbelief in her voice a tad insulting.

"We need to get past this."

She released a sigh full of pain and betrayal and plopped her chin into her cupped hands. "I guess I always knew, what with me being psychic and all."

"I'm sure you did."

"You must be Nannette," Ruthie said.

"Annette," she said, forlornly.

"Can I call you Nan?"

"No. How does she get to be a witch? And a charmling to boot? I'm the one with psychic abilities."

"Trust me, it was a surprise to everyone. Even your mother, Deph."

"Did this danger have anything to do with her death?"

She lowered her head. "I'm afraid so. Your mother died protecting you from another witch trying to confiscate your powers."

A tremor rushed through the house at that, and I got the feeling Percival was upset by that fact, too. I wondered if it happened in the house. If he witnessed it.

A wave of anxiety washed over me at the thought of my mother dying to protect me. That I would be the cause of her death. "Okay. Um." It was my turn to make the timeout sign. "I'm just going to need a minute."

"Sweetheart, we have to hurry."

"No, I know. I just—Give me a sec."

"No!"

Annette and I both jumped then turned slowly to gape at the elegant lady on the screen. She stood up, her jaw set, her eyes shooting fire. Not literally.

"I have not spent the last forty years apart from you, my beloved granddaughter, for you to be slaughtered now. If they come, Defiance—and they will come—they will kill you in the blink of an eye, and then they will drain every ounce of energy, every ounce of magic, you have in your heart."

I lowered myself onto the chair. Annette did the same.

"This is your birthright, Defiance. I deserve more time with you, damn it."

Being scolded by one's grandmother was . . . well, it was kind of awesome. Also, I didn't want to die.

"What do I have to do?"

"You can start by making this symbol. We'll go from there."

"What does that symbol do?"

She bit her lip and studied the paper she held up. "I can't be entirely certain because, again, it's not my language, but if my research has paid off, it will do one of two things: cast you inside a cloak of protection that no mortal being can break or, and this is the kicker, summon an army of demons. Only one way to find out."

"Okay," I said, resigned.

Three hours later, the only thing I had to show for my efforts was a sore arm. We had gotten exactly nowhere. Not that I knew where we were supposed to get to.

I was no closer to figuring out if I could keep Percy. Or Ink. Or Roane. Mostly Roane. And I was no closer to becoming a magician, though I did make an entire plate of spaghetti and meatballs disappear, much to Ruthie's distress.

"Does he come with the house?" I asked her as Annette and I ate. She'd ordered an Italian sub. We figured, since it was quite possible that I'd die in the next few days, there was no reason to go easy on the carbs. "Roane?"

"See, this is why we aren't getting anywhere." She was

busy drawing something. Probably another stupid symbol. Where did she even get pen and paper in the afterlife? "You aren't taking any of this seriously."

"Sure, I am," I said, slurping up my last few strands. "I'm just not sure what I'm supposed to be doing."

"Your powers have been dormant for a long time. They're still there, we just have to figure out how to restart them."

"Oh, what's with all these people coming to the door wanting me to find things for them?"

She looked up. "What?"

"People. Coming to the door. Wanting me to find things. I can barely find my phone when I need it, and nine times out of ten, it's already in my other hand."

"Who's coming to the door?"

"There was a woman a couple houses down," Annette said. "Dark hair. Freckles. Very pretty."

"Dana. Did she lose her wedding ring again?"

"Yep. Then a guy came to the house saying his girlfriend has been missing for over a week."

"Oh, yes. I heard about that."

"Then the banker," I added. "No idea what he wanted. I didn't give him a chance to tell me."

"Mr. Bourne?"

"What gives, Ruthie? Why do they think I can find things?"

She cleared her throat and fanned her face with the papers she'd been drawing on. "That was my specialty."

I got up to wash my plate. I stopped to look at her. She was hiding something.

"It's how I made my living for the most part. Well, that and séances. People simply adore séances."

Annette, who'd been about to fall asleep on top her

Italian sub—one could only take so much of me waving my arm around for no reason whatsoever—perked up. "Séances? You held séances?"

"Yes. Percival was a huge help with that. They were always a big hit."

"Were they real?" she asked. "Could you talk to the dead?"

"I can now." Ruthie giggled at her own joke. "But, for the most part, that kind of thing veered into dark territory, so I tried to stay away from it."

I stood in the center of the room and began making the symbol again.

"Okay, stop before you put an eye out," she said, disgusted.

"This is getting us nowhere. Shouldn't I be learning spells? I mean, isn't there a book or something?"

"A book? A book?" She leaned forward, her piercing gaze razor-sharp. "You can't handle the book." Then she broke down into a fit of giggles, the sound deep and husky like her voice. "I've always wanted to say that. No, but really, you can't. It would be like giving a toddler the detonator to a nuclear warhead."

"That's not insulting at all."

"It shouldn't be. You, my dear, are the nuclear warhead. Remember, you're a source. I think you should master your own magics first, then move on to the more general stuff."

"Maybe I just need a kick start. Something to rekindle the black magic woman in me."

"You know what? Maybe you're right. Maybe you need more motivation. Apparently, not dying a horrible death at the hands of a blood-thirsty warlock is not going to do it. Go to my room and grab the book out of my nightstand."

"Warlocks are a real thing?" I asked.

"They're just witches who use their power for evil."

"Oh, so like Annette."

She jerked awake again. "I do not use my powers for evil."

"Tenth grade. You told Star Furlong you had a premonition she was going to die in a horrible accident if she went to the Smashing Pumpkins concert and you went in her place. With her date."

She sucked air in through her teeth. "Oh, yeah."

"Does that make her a warlock, Grandma?" I asked as I walked out of the room.

I trudged up the stairs—my knees were not what they used to be—did a quick sweep for Roane to no avail, then went to the nightstand and found not one, but two leather-bound books in the drawer, both handmade and ancient. I drew in a breath and ran my fingers over the lettering of the largest. Grimoire.

I hurried downstairs, picking up a stray on the way named Ink, and burst into the kitchen, books in hand.

"Ruthie, these are magnificent. I love old books. I make them for my Etsy store."

She sniffed and patted her nose with a handkerchief. "I know, sweetheart. I've bought a few. Exquisite work."

My jaw dropped to the floor. I picked it back up and sat down with the books. "Are you okay?"

"Yes. I'm wonderful."

"Is that what I think it is?" Annette asked, oohing and aahing over the book as well.

"An authentic grimoire. One of only a couple dozen to survive the witch trials. Open it."

I shook my head. "I need gloves. This book is priceless."

"It's okay."

"Let me at least wash my hands."

She waited while Annette and I both washed and dried our hands.

"What do you do there when you aren't talking to us, Ruthie?" I asked.

"Oh, I have lots of friends here.

"What about my mom?" I asked, suddenly excited. "Could I see her, too?"

"No, honey. This took a ton of preparation for me to do. It would have to have been done before she died."

"Right."

We sat back down and I opened it to the first page. It smelled like dust and old leather and crumbling parchment and it called to me. It seemed to summon my soul right out of my body.

The pages were thick, much thicker than what was used today.

"A grimoire is like a witch's bible," Annette said, her voice filled with awe. "It has all kinds of information that's useful to us."

I almost cracked up then figured who was I to judge? If she wanted to embrace the life with me, I was more than happy to have her along.

She continued as we flipped through the pages. They were brittle and I feared for their safety.

"Look. It has the lunar phases. Color correspondences. Herb correspondences. Info about the sabbath. And, see?" She poked one of the fragile pages and I winced. "Spells!"

"You need to study that," Ruthie said. "You'll need to know all of it. But don't forget." She pointed to the book. "Detonator." Then to me. "Nuclear warhead."

"Got it. What about this one?" I showed her the other book I found. A journal, though it looked just as old as the grimoire.

She smiled. "That one is the motivation."

I opened it. "The pages are empty."

"Exactly. That is my personal book of shadows."

Annette gasped. It was a long, drawn out thing that teetered somewhere between melodrama and soul-crushing hysteria.

"I take it you know what that means?" I asked.

She nodded like a kid in a candy store when asked, "Which flavor is your favorite?" Only in Annette's case, a tequila store.

"It's a witch's journal. A lot of people think grimoires and books of shadows are the same thing, but they're not."

"You're right, Nannette." Ruthie looked pleased with her. At least someone could put a smile on her face. Though I could hardly be jealous of Nannette. I did love her so.

"Right. I knew that," I said, lying through my pearly whites.

"Liar."

"The pages only look empty. I don't want just anyone reading my personal journal. However, if you really want to, you can. You know how."

"More symbols?" I asked, infusing my voice with way more whine than I normally used.

"I know you're tired and overwhelmed, but we have to do something. Open the book of shadows and try to read it."

I did as she ordered, and so began another session of a whole lot of nothing.

"Am I supposed to draw the symbol over the paper?"

"I don't know, hon. I just know that charmlings can read all books of shadows, no matter how strong the magics are that bind them. It's supposed to be one of your gifts."

"Ruthie, are you sure I am this thing? I'm a charmling? I mean, I've never done magic in my life."

"Oh, honey, trust me. You've done magic."

That got my attention. "When?"

"From the time you were born. I didn't send you into hiding until you were three. Before that, you were the most powerful being I'd ever had the honor of being in the presence of." She showed me another drawing. "What about this symbol? Does it mean anything to you? Spark any memories?"

Disappointment enveloped me and I deflated like a balloon with a slow leak. "No. What does it mean?"

"No idea. I just saw it on a document once."

"So, it could be a logo for a European car company for all you know?"

"Actually, yes."

Annette was now snoring on the table, her glasses askew on her face, her mouth twisted to the side. She was also drooling, but only a little.

"I'm beat, too."

"No!" Ruthie said, jumping to her feet.

"You may not need sleep, but I do. I'm going to bed." I started to get up, then I stopped and asked, "Wait. Do you need sleep?"

"I don't think so. I have another call to make anyway."

"A call? Who are you calling this late at night?"

"Just meditate on all of this before you go to sleep, okay? It's in there, Dephne. We just have to find it."

"I will. I promise. But I do have another question. Why did you think the books would motivate me?"

"Books have always been your motivation. Even when you were a toddler. The older, the better."

She was right. That knowledge—the knowledge that she knew such intimate things about me—filled me with warmth.

"Night, Ruthie."

"Night, sweetheart." She looked worried. I hadn't managed to muster a spark of magic much less master the whole of witchcraft in a single night.

Even worried, she was beautiful. I'd give her that. If not for that slight touch of Nora Desmond, she'd almost pass for normal. Ish.

I gathered my BFF and herded her up the stairs to Ruthie's bedroom. I'd no more laid my head down before I heard a soft knock on the front door.

"Not again."

I slipped on a robe and tip-toed to the first floor, hoping to peek out without the visitor seeing me. It was my neighbor Parris Hampton.

I cracked the door open. "Parris, is everything okay?"

"Oh, no. You were in bed. I'm so sorry, Defiance. I'll come back tomorrow."

"No, no, it's okay. Do you need anything?"

"Heavens no. I was just going to see how you're doing. And I brought wine."

"Well, get in here." I waved her inside.

"What's going on?" Annette asked from the balcony as she rubbed her eyes.

"Wine."

She awoke like a rocket. "I'll get the glasses."

SIX

Sing like no one is listening.
Dance like you need to be shot
with a tranquilizer dart.
-Meme

The second Parris stepped across the threshold carrying a bottle of Moscato the walls quaked around us.

"Percy," I said under my breath, scowling at him. "Be nice." He shuddered again, quick and short, like a dog shaking its fur. "Thank you."

For the first time, I turned on a few lights in the great room and took the sheets off some of the furniture.

Ink joined us on the couch, flicking his tail anytime anyone tried to touch him, which we did often. He was a cat. A creature of the animal genus Felis catus. What did he expect?

Annette came back with wine glasses and took the charcoal gray wingback.

After some getting-to-know-you chitchat, I steered the conversation toward my grandmother. "Can you tell me more about her?" I asked Parris.

About my age, Parris had long chestnut hair that had been through a few too many colorings and a pretty face that'd already seen the sharp end of a Botox syringe. At least she wasn't a tanning-bed aficionado like her husband. I very much wanted to ask her more about their living arrangements even though it was none of my business.

"What was she like? Did you know her well?"

"Not as well as I'd liked. She was a firecracker, Defiance. Told it like it was."

Her words brought a smile to my insides and out.

"She talked about you all the time."

"Really?" I said in awe. Ruthie knew so much about me. Everything, apparently. Yet I'd known nothing about her.

"That's so strange," Annette said, already into her third glass with hardly a slur in site. Girl could put 'em away. "How much she knew about you, Deph."

"Why is that?" Parris asked.

I didn't know why, but I felt I should keep the whole never-met-my-grandmother card close to my chest. I was a witch, after all. I needed to learn to trust my instincts. Every time I ignored them, I got burned. Case in point, my snake-skinned ex and his reptilian mother.

Annette looked at me for a clue as to how to proceed, her expression apologetic. I shook my head dismissively, and said, "We just didn't get to see that much of each other. She kept up with my life better than I kept up with hers."

Parris nodded and shifted her position, and I could tell she was fishing. That was okay. I liked fishing, too.

"So," she said after taking another sip of her Moscato

and flipping her hair over her shoulder in complete nonchalance, "um, are you like her?"

"In what way?" I asked, knowing exactly what she meant.

Annette hid a grin behind her glass.

"You know, can you, I don't know, do the things she could do?"

I decided to alleviate her anticipation. "Not as far as I know, but the day is young, as they say."

She straightened her shoulders in interest. "Then you're entering the religion?"

"Considering it."

"I think you should. If you have half the talent your grandmother did . . . let's just say, that woman was all kinds of amazing."

I nodded and thought of the people I'd met so far. "I've been hearing that a lot."

"Let me know how it goes. I love a good séance. Do all witches perform séances?"

That was a great question. "I have to admit, Parris, I don't know that much about it, yet."

"Oh, no worries. I was just wondering. It's all so fascinating."

"I agree."

"Speaking of fascinating," she said, leaning closer. "What about the fabulous Mr. Wildes?"

"Roane?" Annette asked. "He's real?"

I gaped at her. "What would make you think he isn't real? I've told you about him. I've described him in Technicolor detail."

She shrugged. "I have to see that kind of stunning to believe it."

"You have no idea what you're missing," Parris said.

"Am I right?"

I laughed. "You are most definitely right."

"After everything that happened to him, and everything he's had to overcome with such a tragic past, it's a miracle he's turned out so well."

"Oh?" I said, scooting closer to her. "What happened exactly?"

"You don't know?" Her eyes glistened with intrigue, but she went to pet Ink and, instead of talking, she gasped when she got a handful of needlelike claws in return. She yelped and pulled back her hand.

"Ink!" I grabbed Parris's hand to get a look, then glared at the mangy creature. "Bad boy."

"It's okay," she said, wresting her hand out of my grip. "Totally my fault. I should probably put something on this." She stood to leave. "It's past midnight anyway."

Disappointment washed over me. I wanted to know more about the fabulous Mr. Wildes and what he went through. What he had to overcome.

Annette and I stood to show her out.

"Thanks for coming over," I said. "This was fun."

She turned and nodded. "It was, wasn't it?"

I laughed softly. "Surprised?"

"Oh, no, it's not that. It's just . . . I don't know. I wasn't sure you'd want to hang with me."

"Why wouldn't I want to hang with you?"

She shrugged. "Insecurity, I guess."

I couldn't imagine a woman like her having such a thing, but we all had our hang-ups.

After one last sweep of the house, she sighed and said dreamily, "I've always loved this house. It has so much personality. So much potential." She took my hand into hers. "If you ever decide to sell, will you please call me first?"

"Sure."

"No, I mean it. I would love to restore Percy to his original glory."

For some reason, that seemed to take a weight off my shoulders. At least if I did end up selling him, I'd know he was going to someone who loved him as much as I did.

"Thank you, Parris. I'll keep that in mind."

TWELVE THOUSAND HOURS LATER, I lay awake beside Annette, staring at the ceiling and listening to her soft snore. I had no clue what to do. One more day to pull out of the contract.

I loved Percy. Who wouldn't? Well, besides Mrs. Richter, who was stark raving. I mean, who was afraid of a house? I didn't get it. He'd been nothing but a gentleman to me.

Since my mind wouldn't shut off, even after two glasses of wine, I decided it wasn't too early for coffee. I slid into a pair of slippers and plodded down to the first floor. Apparently, my sleeping habits resembled those of a bear. I either slept for days at a time or not at all.

After pouring a cup, I sat at the breakfast table to check my email. Ink joined me, curling up first in my lap and then eventually on my laptop. Because that was helpful. I laid my arm across the table, resting my head on it, and used my free hand pet him. He let me, even going so far as to sniff my nose and mouth, his whiskers tickling as he inspected his latest acquaintance.

"I bet you have a ton of girlfriends, don't you, big guy?"

His battle scars would suggest he'd gotten into plenty of fights over them.

I thought about bringing up the grandma app but had no idea if she was asleep. Or if she needed sleep. Gawd, I would get so much more done if I didn't need sleep. The fine lines that had started forming around my eyes loved it when I didn't get sleep, though, and I loathed giving them any reason to celebrate their existence.

With Ink purring beside me, I let my lids drift shut. The surreal swam up to meet me just as a knock sounded at the front door. I jerked awake.

This. Was. Not. Happening.

I decided a *No Trespassing* sign would not do the trick. I was going to buy yellow crime scene tape and crisscross it over the door. I might even toss some red paint here and there in a random, blood-splatter-esque pattern. Really freak people out. Give them pause before knocking, especially at . . . I looked at my bare wrist again . . . whatever o'clock in the morning.

I opened the door to an older gentleman. He had to be in his late seventies and wore that same look of panic I'd seen too often in the last couple of days. I was coming to despise that look. It would be one thing if I could help these people. It was an entirely different kind of agony knowing there was nothing I could do.

The man blinked at me in surprise, then asked, "Is Ruthie home?"

Oh, no. I had to give him the news. This was going to suck. I thought everyone knew. "I'm sorry. Ruthie passed away a few days ago."

I didn't think my words sank in at first. He looked confused and then . . . and then devastated. Like I'd just told him he only had five minutes to live.

"No," he whispered, stumbling back. "Please, no."

I lunged forward to steady him. "Why don't you come in. Let's get you some water."

He let me lead him all the way back to the kitchen.

After setting him at the table, I grabbed a glass and a bottle of water out of the fridge. "Here you go."

"She's gone?" he asked, his eyes watering, his dusky skin reddening.

"I'm so sorry." I sat beside him.

"I need her help." The look on his face brought tears to my eyes.

"Maybe I can do something." I could've kicked myself. There was not a damned thing I could do, yet the desire to alleviate this man's pain was overwhelming.

As though noticing me for the first time, he brought a hand up to my face and brushed his fingertips over my cheek. "You're Defiance, aren't you? You look just like her."

"Just like her?"

"Ruthie. She told me all about you. You have the same eyes. The same mouth."

For some reason, his statement brought on a rush of elation. I'd never looked like anyone before in my life. Some people would tell me I looked like one of my dads, or even both, but that wasn't a real resemblance. We weren't blood relatives.

"Thank you. What's going on, Mr. . . . ?"

"Touma. I'm Jameel."

I took his hand. "It's nice to meet you. Can you tell me what happened?"

"My wife, Siham. She's missing. She has Alzheimer's and sometimes gets out of the house."

That sickly dread I'd been feeling so much of lately crept up my spine again, like a giant spider under my shirt.

"Usually, I find her immediately. Not this time. I've searched everywhere. It's so cold out." He covered my hands with his, his red-rimmed eyes brimming with unspent tears. "I was asleep. I don't even know how long she's been gone." A tear finally broke free and slid down his dusky cheek. "But you can do it, too, yes? You can . . . find things?"

I closed my eyes, drew in a deep breath, then opened them again. "Mr. Touma, I am so sorry. I don't have the same skillset my grandmother had."

He shook his head. "No, she told me you'd eventually take over. She said you're more skilled than even she is. More powerful than anything she's ever seen."

My jaw locked shut. How in blazing saddles could Ruthie say such a thing? She didn't even know me. I could've lost whatever talent I had. Whatever talent she thought I had. How could she give people such false hope?

"Mr. Touma, have you called the police?"

"Yes. Of course, but Ruthie always . . ." He stood. His movements slow as though he were in shock, he started toward the door. I followed him.

"I am so sorry. I hope they find her, Mr. Touma."

The look he gave me, the agonizing gaze he lobbed my way, crushed my heart and lungs.

I was going to kill her.

AS SOON AS I saw Mr. Touma to his car, the icy air slicing through the thin veil of my pajamas and into my flesh, I hurried back inside, strode to the kitchen where my laptop sat, and opened the app.

She was dead. She was already dead, yes. Now she was deader. I was going to see to it.

I brought up the video and opened my mouth to yell, but she was gone. I sat down, stunned. The video showed only a white screen and nothing else.

"Ruthie?" I asked, my tone wary. I waited. Nothing. Then I panicked. "Ruthie!"

After a minute, she stumbled onto the screen, unkempt, her hair in disarray. Did that mean the departed did sleep?

"Where have you been?" I asked in a state of near panic.

She looked around. "Right here. Where else would I be?"

"You weren't there."

"I had things to do."

"Grandma, you are stuck inside the veil, apparently for all eternity. What could you possibly have to do?"

After a quick glance of surprise—why she would be surprised by my outburst, I had no idea—she recovered with the barest hint of a smile, and said, "Well, I do have a life, Defiance." She brushed lint off her clothes and sniffed. "Or, I did."

"You told Mr. Touma I was taking over for you." My tone was not gentle. Nor quiet.

"I told everyone you were taking over for me."

"Why would you do that?" I grabbed my hair and dropped my forehead onto the table. "Why would you give people false hope?"

"You?" she asked with a snort. "False hope? Defiance Tiffany Dayne, I keep telling you—"

"Yes, yes, I know." I looked up at her. "I'm a witch. I get it even though thus far we have seen exactly bupkis of my supposed skills. And now the entire town thinks I'm the second coming."

Her expression softened. "Sweetheart, what happened?"

"Mr. Touma. That's what happened. And I can't help him."

"Oh, no. Mrs. Touma?"

"Yes. Wait." I let go of my hair and straightened. "You do it. You can find her, right? I mean, you're dead. Can't you guys move through walls and stuff?"

"No, Defiance, it doesn't work that way. I mean, maybe. All I know is that I can't just cross the veil. That's why I had to create the spell. So I could communicate with you."

"Then you're stuck on the other side?"

"For now. Even if I could cross, there's no guarantee I could see you. It's different here."

"What can I do?" I asked, miserable. I couldn't go on like this. People coming to me for help and me being about as useful as a screen door on a submarine.

"You can do this, Dephne. I know you can."

"Ruthie—"

"No. No more second-guessing. Keep hold of that emotion. That feeling of powerlessness."

"Oh, that baby's not going anywhere. I guarantee it."

"Good. Now, take that emotion and turn it. Use it, Defiance. Bend it to your will."

"You mean, like, make it my bitch?"

She covered her mouth with a delicate hand and coughed, then said, "Yes, sweetheart. Make it your bitch."

"Who are you making your bitch?" Annette asked, shuffling into the kitchen and rubbing her eyes. "God, it's so bright." She shoved her glasses on. They sat crooked on her adorable nose, and her mop of brown hair, which had been pulled into a ponytail, stuck out in every direction imaginable. She stopped and frowned at me. "What time is it?"

"Coffee time for me. You go back to bed."

"Nope. I'm here for you. That's what besties are for. I'll make the coffee. How much wine did I have?"

"Enough for both of us."

"Figures. I never could turn down a good Moscato."

I watched her shuffle to the pot, my mind resembling her hair, going in every direction imaginable. In every direction except the one it needed to go.

"Ruthie, what if I can't do this?" I chewed on a nail for a few seconds, then said what I was sure everyone was thinking. "What if it's gone?"

"Defiance," she said, her voice soft, "look at me."

I looked.

"Stop chewing your nails."

I dropped my hand.

"I want you to do something for me."

"'Kay."

"There's a silver tray on the hutch in the dining room. Go get it and bring it here."

"'Kay."

After uncovering the hutch, I found a silver tray with a silver tea set atop it. I cleared it off and brought the tray back. "Got it."

"Make sure you can see your reflection in it, then prop it up against something."

I braced it against the napkin holder.

Annette sat beside me, once again pushing a cup of coffee across to me. "Is this some kind of spell?" she asked.

"No. This is some kind of kick in the seat. A kickstart, if you will. What do you see?"

After releasing a lungful of air, I shrugged. "I see me."

"No. Actually, my love, you don't. What do you see?"

"Okay, me only distorted."

"Nope again."

"Ruthie, I don't understand." I draped my arms over the table and rested my head in the crook of an elbow.

"What do you see? Describe that woman to me."

I lifted my head again, pressed my mouth together, and studied the woman in the mirror. Analyzed all of her flaws. All of her shortcomings. Sadly, there were a lot. "I see a woman who's so broke she doesn't know where her next meal is coming from."

"Better. What else?"

"I see a woman so stupid, she let a backstabbing snake steal everything she's ever worked for right out from under her."

"What else?"

"I see a talentless wannabe who's out of luck, out of shape, and running out of time."

"And that, my dear, is why you can't summon your powers."

"Right. I get it. I just need to see the beautiful person inside and love her for who she is and all my dreams will come true?"

"Not at all."

"Oh, thank God." I didn't need a pep talk from my dearly departed grandmother, no matter how awesome she was.

"Defiance Dayne *is* a beautiful person. Inside and out. But she needs to shut up, sit down, and pay attention to the other thing lingering in her periphery. That thing she sent to the corner. Hid in the darkest recesses of her mind. You know exactly which one I'm talking about. The thing you are most afraid of because it is so dark and so bright and so powerful, it will change everything you've ever known about the world you live in. And change, my dear, good or bad, is scary."

"I've heard that," Annette said from behind her cup.

"Now, tell me again what you see, only let the thing come out and play. What does it see?"

For some insanely bizarre reason, everything she just said made perfect sense.

"Let it get a good look. What do you see, now?"

"I see a woman so broke, she has nowhere to go but up."

I saw her smile in my periphery. "What else?"

"I see a woman who let a backstabbing snake steal everything she's ever worked for right out from under her, so she has to work doubly hard to rebuild her life and take back what she's owed."

She crossed her arms, her chin rising. "What else?"

I gazed at the distorted reflection. Slowed my breathing. Decelerated my heartbeats. The world fell from beneath my feet, and I heard my grandmother's voice from somewhere far away.

"What else, Defiance? What else do you see?"

"I see a woman born of royal blood who can bend luck to her will. Who can shape matter as she pleases. Who can command time to do her bidding."

"And what would you do, Defiance Dayne, to help those who need you most?"

My voice, though I recognized it, seemed to come from somewhere else. I lowered my head, gazed into my own eyes, and spoke words I had not said since I was a kid. "I would set the world on fire."

And then, as though someone else were controlling me, something else, I raised a hand to the tray and drew a symbol with two fingers, my movements automatic. The symbol was none of those Ruthie showed me. This one was different. But I knew it to the depths of my being.

Power.

It flowed through my fingers, sparking and cracking the fabric of reality. Light bled from each line I drew until the symbol was complete and a power like I'd never felt before exploded inside me.

My soul, the very essence of my being, caught fire.

I couldn't see it was so bright. I couldn't hear it was so loud. Flames rushed through me, burning me from the inside out.

What no one had bothered to mention, which in hindsight would have been nice, was that it hurt. This power waiting in the darkness. No wonder I sent it to stand in the corner. It scorched every cell in my body. The pain was so fierce, I couldn't catch my breath. I was strapped to an electric chair that no one would turn off.

I fell to the ground and stumbled to the stairs. I needed cold. I needed ice and snow and then a really good salve because this was going to leave a mark.

Someone was screaming and I realized it was me, only I was screaming from somewhere else. From another plane of existence. I thought that odd since I was clearly on this one. Maybe my voice was bouncing through space and time. Or my soul was trying to escape the body in which it was trapped.

My knees hit the stairs as I stumbled up them, tripping on every single one.

I reached the bathroom then fell again. I just wanted to feel the rush of cold water. To soothe. To douse the flames.

Before I could crawl another inch, I felt my consciousness slipping away. The tile floor felt good against my face. But it wasn't enough. I was going to burn to death. I knew it.

Then I felt arms around me. They lifted me off the floor.

"Water," I said to whomever had picked me up. "Cold."

The shower curtains were shoved aside and I was lifted over the edge of the clawfoot. Strong hands turned the handles and water, sweet icy water, washed over me.

I lifted my face to the frigid streams and heard him. Roane. He held me upright from behind and spoke softly into my ear, his warm breath fanning across my cheek.

"You're okay."

His arms were like a vise around me. Firm. Unyielding. The length of his body against mine was almost as soothing as the cold water.

I lay my head back against his shoulder and let the water douse the wildfire inside me.

"You're okay," he said again, his voice as smooth as Tennessee whiskey.

I wrapped my arms over his and sank against him. His hold tightened and he pulled me closer, his mouth brushing over my ear and along my cheek. He just held me there under the stream of icy water, getting soaked himself.

And then it hit me like the boulder in a Roadrunner cartoon. It was real. It was all real. Everything Ruthie had said, no matter how unfathomable. It was all real.

A part of me never believed it. A part of me wondered if Ruthie weren't still alive somewhere, perhaps Skyping from a villa in France. Yet here I was, being held by a god while he ran cold tap water in the physical world over the flames that had engulfed me in the spiritual one.

An emotion spread throughout my body; I just didn't know which one it was. Amazement? Disbelief? Elation? All of the above?

My chest swelled with both relief and dread. I straightened and turned to him. Water dripped down his face. He smoothed back his hair with one hand, keeping me steady with the other.

"It's all real," I said.

He nodded, a knowing expression softening the concerned lines on his face. "It is."

"How is that even possible?"

The grin that lifted one corner of his mouth set me on fire once again, only this time it was concentrated in my nether regions. "I only work here, beautiful."

I let out a breathy laugh.

He called me beautiful.

Then I realized he was fully clothed. As was I. Both of us soaking wet.

"Oh, my God, I'm so sorry." I pushed open the curtain and reached for a towel, only almost toppling over three times to get to it. Thankfully, he had yet to let go.

I draped the towel over his head and patted his face dry before smoothing it over his hair. It sat around his shoulders like a boxer coming out for a fight.

Then I grabbed his shoulders and gazed into his eyes. "Please, for the love of all things holy, tell me this isn't going to ruin your kilt."

He laughed under his breath. "It'll be fine."

Thank you, Jesus.

"Better?" he asked.

I nodded.

He turned off the water then took the towel from around his neck and dried my face, brushing it softly over my skin. Then he squeezed my hair with it, ringing out most of the water.

He had to reach around me to do so, and I put my hands on his chest to steady myself. His mouth was gorgeous, his lips fuller than most male's and sculpted to absolute perfection. I reached up and ran my fingertips along them.

Surprised, he stopped and looked down at me through lashes spiked with wetness. The effect shot hot daggers straight to my abdomen.

Slowly, as though he wanted to savor the moment, he bent his head, his lips coming close enough to mine to feel the electricity arc between us.

Then he stopped. His brows cinched together and he raised up, tilting his head to the side. "Your grandmother. She's calling to you."

I listened, too. Heard nothing. Still . . . "I guess I better get back down there."

He nodded, but before I could move, he lifted me in his arms and over the edge to set me down on a chenille rug. He climbed out without letting me go to make sure I had my footing.

"Thank you," I said, the words so hollow they echoed. How did one thank someone for saving their life?

He wrapped the towel around my shoulders. "Don't mention it. I'd be glad to help you shower any time."

A zing rushed through me and I knew I had to get out of there before I attacked him. I hurried toward the door but couldn't help a quick glance over my shoulder for one more look. The wet T-shirt that was molded to the hills and valleys of his muscles was something to see. If I ever opened a bar, I was totally hosting wet T-shirt contests.

He tilted his head as though curious why I would look at him like that. I'd have to explain it to him someday.

SEVEN

I'm a middle-aged woman with an Etsy store.
I have hot flashes and a rotary cutter.
Any questions?
-T-shirt

I hurried downstairs, my slippers sloshing on the wood floors, which couldn't be good for them.

"Grandma?" I said when I got to the kitchen.

"Oh, Defiance." She was in tears, her hands covering her mouth.

"Are you okay?" I asked.

"Are *you* okay?"

"I am. I just . . . got really hot."

"I've never seen anything like that." She pressed her hands to her chest. "Thank you, my darling girl, for letting me witness what few will ever see in their lifetime."

"A woman on fire?"

"The rebirth of a true, blood-born charmling."

"You couldn't have mentioned the fire?"

"I've just never seen . . . That was . . ." She waved a hand over her face. "You were magnificent."

"Most people on fire are."

I finally glanced at Annette. She was holding a cup of coffee in both hands, only her eyes visible over the rim, and they were saucers.

"Annette?" I slid into the seat next to her. "Annette, talk to me."

Her gaze slowly shifted my way. "I don't know if you're aware of this, but I don't think most witches can do that."

"No. No, they can't," Ruthie said. "However, you just sent up a beacon. They'll know where you are now. You must raise the protection spell. You must diffuse the foot-print of your energy, or every witch powerful enough to feel it will be knocking on your door. Most will only want to meet you. Others, however, will stop at nothing to take it. And the hunters . . ." She gave a delicate shudder.

"Can I dry off first?"

A breathy laugh escaped her. "Yes. Also, that took a lot of energy. You need to rest, but only for a couple of hours, okay?"

I'd just been burned alive. I wasn't sure how much rest I would get. With electricity crackling through me, both painful and exhilarating, I walked upstairs, hoping to catch another glimpse of tall, dark, and inked. I had to ask myself why he was here in the wee hours of morn. He always seemed to appear out of nowhere then disappear just as mysteriously.

I searched the second floor for him where he'd been working on the bathrooms. Nothing. No sign of any other living being besides Ink, who sat on Ruthie's bed with a come-hither stare, tail wagging seductively, and Annette, who sat on Ruthie's bed with a blank stare, no tail wagging, seductively or otherwise. Which was a shame, really.

"You okay, Nette?"

She'd leaned back against the headboard, her back stiff, her face void of emotion. "I'm okay," she said, her voice feigning lightness.

I tried to stroke Ink's fur. He was apparently feeling feisty. He went into attack mode, twisted onto his back, and sank his teeth and claws into my flesh. I sucked a sharp breath in through my teeth and tried to dislodge him. It was like pulling out cactus needles.

Annette sat oblivious. I had to do something. To snap her out of it. I thought about slapping her like they did in the movies but thought better of it. Mostly because she could kick my ass.

I cleared my throat instead and said as nonchalantly as possible, "Roane took a shower with me."

She jerked out of her stupor so fast I worried she'd get whiplash. "What?"

I fought a giggle.

"What did you say?"

"That spell thing burned."

She wilted. "Yes. I heard the screams."

"He helped me into the shower, only he got in, too. To hold me steady."

Guilt commandeered the lines on her face. She lowered her head and studied the comforter, smoothing it with her fingertips. "I should have come to help you, Deph. I heard the screams and I did nothing."

"Nette, don't you dare put that on yourself. There was nothing you could have done."

"I was just . . . I was so stunned. I couldn't move."

"You were in shock."

"No, it was like I was paralyzed."

"Maybe the spell had something to do with it."

"It must have because I honestly couldn't move. I was shocked, yes, but you were screaming and I just sat there. Being shocked. It's not like me."

"No, it's not." I put a hand on her shoulder. "It wasn't your fault. There was nothing you could've done."

"Wait, he got in, too?"

My mouth widened. "He did."

"Did he happen to get naked first?"

"Sadly, no. We both got drenched."

She scooted down until her head was on her pillow. "How did drenched look on him?"

I graced her with a devilish grin, one that would leave little doubt in her mind. Just in case, however, I added, "You have no idea."

"Oh, man. I have got to see this guy. Wait!" She bolted upright and leveled a pleading stare on me. "Is the . . . is the kilt okay?"

I laughed out loud.

"Please, tell me it's okay."

We thought so much alike. "He says it'll be fine. But we might want to find a kilt store to make sure we have a backup."

She waved a dismissive hand. "We're good. I have several bookmarked. So, like, where is he? Does he have his own house? Why was he here so early?"

"I have no idea." I sat nibbling on a hangnail. "I've been wondering that myself. I may have to get the lowdown on our mysterious Mr. Wildes from Ruthie."

"Good idea." Her lids sat at half-mast as sleep took over. "She's kind of amazing."

"I agree."

Her breathing evened out instantly, which was hilarious since Ink had decided her hair was a multifaceted chew toy.

I reached over, removed her glasses, and put them on the nightstand where I'd put Ruthie's book of shadows. I set it on my lap and opened it to run my fingers over a couple of pages. If she did write in it, her pen left no indentions. Maybe I could find a recipe to reveal invisible ink online. Until then, I decided to give it my best shot.

Granted, the first time I actually succeeded in creating magics did not go well and a blinding pain consumed me for what seemed like an eternity, surely it wouldn't be like that every time. If so, magic sucked.

Zero stars.

Would not recommend.

Keeping in mind that this was my grandmother's journal where her most private thoughts were written, her darkest secrets recorded, I wanted to treat the artifact with the respect it deserved.

I wanted to. I did not succeed.

The thought of uncovering information about my only living-up-until-a-few-days-ago relative had me positively giddy. But according to said woman, I needed to rest. To prepare for the protection spell. It would take a lot out of me.

As long as it didn't light me on fire, I'd be good as gold.

I glanced out the massive window. Dawn was just beginning to bleed across the horizon, and I had yet to sleep a wink. Still, no time like the present to uncover the past.

I just had to figure out what symbol to use. I was supposedly born knowing the charmling language. Surely, like the protection spell, it would magically pop into my head. Because, while I may have been born knowing the language, I lost that knowledge along with memories of cutting my first set of teeth and the horrific details of my birth. Some things were better left forgotten.

Playing a less lethal form of Russian Roulette, I flipped through the journal and stopped on a random page.

This was it. This would be the true test. Could I do this one on my own? Could I show what had been hidden?

Even as I thought the words, an image began to form.

Reveal.

I realized it really was a language. While most magics used a spoken form of delivery for manifestation, like with spells and such, charmling magic used something much older. The symbols were basically the same spells, only in a single word using an ancient form of pictographs. Like Egyptian hieroglyphs or Chinese characters. Where a symbol was used to represent a word or even an entire phrase.

This knowledge unfolded in my head like I'd opened a book in my mind, and everything I needed to know was inside. Only parts of it were blurry. Parts of it made no sense. And parts of it were downright dark, deliberately covered in shadows and fog. It would take a lot more to reveal those than what I had to offer at the moment.

The one I was looking for stood out, as though magnified in bold font on the page. The lines glowing. The edges razor sharp. And my hand took over.

I drew the shape over the page with two fingers, my movements automatic. The lines caught fire. Light seeped out of them as I drew each streak, each loop with infinite care. It scorched the air, yet I couldn't tell if the light was real or only in my mind. If anyone besides me could see it.

The fire I'd felt before, the blistering electricity, ignited and rushed over my skin, though not nearly as powerfully as before. The pain was manageable as I completed the symbol. It was only after I'd finished that I realized I'd bitten down so hard my jaw ached. My left hand had gripped the edge of the book so tightly my fingers trembled. And every muscle in my body had constricted to the point of rigor mortis.

It worked, though. Letters began seeping through the paper. Words began forming. A date. A place. A name.

The words shocked me. What I read surprised me to such a degree that I lost what little concentration I'd had, and the ink began to disappear. I read it again as quickly as I could, but only managed to decipher one complete sentence. A single line that changed everything.

According to her own journal, my grandmother had been accused of murder. Of killing a man. And if I read that next line correctly before it disappeared, she was guilty.

I slammed the book shut so hard the room quaked. Either that or I woke up Percy.

"Sorry, Percy," I whispered to him.

Thankfully my reaction didn't faze Annette. Though it did manage to scare poor Ink half to death. He tore off the bed and sprinted down the hall as I sat gaping into oblivion. Murder? My grandmother? My mind could not reconcile those two concepts.

I slipped out of bed and walked to the stairs, only I was starting to feel a bit woozy. The edges of my vision blurred then darkened and I remembered thinking how pretty the wood floor was right before my face hit it.

I WOKE up on the sofa with a throw pillow underneath my head and a warm cloth on top of it. I bolted upright, paused to let the world stop spinning, then hurried to the kitchen.

Then I smelled food. Eggs frying and bacon sizzling and bread toasting. My mouth watered and I entered the kitchen fully prepared to beg for a bite. I was not above selling my soul to the chef.

Roane stood in front of the industrial stove in an army green T-shirt and his requisite kilt. This one was darker than the one he'd been wearing. Almost black.

"Ms. Dayne," he said without turning around. "Breakfast?"

"Did I pass out or something?"

"Or something. How do you like your eggs?"

That was a tough one. On the one hand, I liked them over medium. On the other, I liked them fertilized. The clock was ticking on my particular egg supply, after all. My storage unit was almost empty if it weren't already.

Still, I didn't want to scare Roane. To send him packing. Percy needed a lot of help.

"Over medium."

"You got it."

"How did I get to the sofa?"

"With help." He scooped two eggs onto a plate with a couple of slices of bacon and some toast, the movement causing his biceps to flex, and I had to tear my gaze off them when he turned toward me.

It was a sad moment in the annals of Defiance the Dayne.

Yet that was the exact moment I realized what a mess I must be. I hadn't done anything to help my appearance since I caught fire a few hours ago. God only knew what my hair looked like. And I could only hope my face wasn't disfigured from the fall.

I smoothed down my hair and took the plate from him. "Thanks."

He gave me a quick once over and every insecurity I'd felt since the day I was born flared up inside me. Seriously, did I really need to wear Frozen pajamas? I hadn't even applied moisturizer. Or mascara. And where was a bra when I needed one?

I ever-so-nonchalantly wrapped my free arm over the girls and sat at the table.

After pouring us both a cup of coffee, he handed mine to me and started to head out. But there were certain things I needed to know. And his disappearing acts were becoming a hindrance to that end.

"Aren't you eating?" I asked.

He paused and turned back but kept his gaze low. I must have looked worse than I thought.

"Already ate."

"Please stay a minute."

He bit down as though weighing the pros and cons, before folding his large frame into a chair across from me.

"You know, Annette thinks you're a figment of my imagination."

A grin that could make a retired nun ovulate brightened his face. "What do you think?"

"I think, luckily for me, you show up at some pretty opportune times."

"So, no?"

"Probably not. Where do you live?"

He took a sip then gave me his full attention. "Close by."

"Vague much?" I asked with a laugh. "What if I need to contact you?"

He reached over, his nearness intoxicating, his scent part laundry soap and part sandalwood, and took my phone. After holding it up to my face to unlock it, he punched in some numbers and gave it back. "Now I'm no farther away than a push of a button."

For reasons I couldn't possibly fathom—as if—that made me giddy.

"Are you feeling better?" he asked.

"Since I caught fire? Or since I fell on my face? Either way, thank you. The fire thing really sucked, though."

He chuckled, the sound husky and alluring. "I'm sure it did. But it worked, right? It did the trick?"

This time I put my fork down and gave him my full attention. "Do you know about me?"

"Your grandmother told me a few things."

"She's living in my computer. Ruthie that is."

"Not sure why, but that doesn't surprise me."

"Want to say hi?"

"I'd love to." Like talking to the dead through some astral version of Google Hangouts was an everyday occurrence. He was openminded. I'd give him that.

I opened my laptop and watched as Ruthie stood motionless beyond the veil. Her blond 'do coiffed to perfection. And, if I didn't know better, I'd say she'd applied lipstick. Roane came around and took the chair beside me, his nearness sending fireworks bursting across my skin, and I hoped it wasn't the magic making another impromptu appearance.

He tilted his head toward mine for a better view and we waited.

And waited.

"Ruthie?" I said after a minute. "What are you doing?"

She stayed stock still. Not moving. Not blinking. Not breathing. But that was probably a given.

"Um, Ruthie? We have company."

"I'm on pause," she said at last.

"I didn't pause you. You're real. There's no pause button on reality."

She grinned. "There is for you, darling girl. Hi, Roane."

"Hi, Mrs. Goode," he said, his voice infused with humor.

"Wait. Doesn't this surprise you?" I asked. He was so nonchalant about it. "I mean, she died. Aren't you a little freaked?"

"Nothing your grandmother does surprises me anymore."

"Mmmm," I mmmed. "I wouldn't be so sure." I stabbed Ruthie with my best accusatory glower. "What about—" I paused for dramatic effect "—*murder*?"

He lifted his gaze and thought a moment. Bouncing back, he said, "Nope. Not that either."

"What are you talking about, Defiance?"

"Your journal."

"My book of shadows?" The shock on her face told me everything I needed to know. She'd done it. She'd really killed someone.

Well, she'd better have a damn good reason or this relationship was coming to a complete and abrupt end.

"That's right. I read it. Well, one page of it. Actually, just a couple of lines, but I read it. You were accused of murder and, according to your own words in your own journal, you were guilty."

She blinked in rapid succession. I'd busted her. What kind of grandmother killed people?

"Defiance," she said, her voice full of awe, "that would take even the most powerful of witches weeks to break. It's like a highly-secured encrypted code that only a supercomputer could break and even then it would take, well, weeks."

"So, I'm like a hacker?"

"You're . . . incredi—"

"Also, I passed out."

"You passed out? It must be the magics."

"But I didn't pass out when I caught fire."

"Maybe the cold water helped," Roane said.

"Yes." Ruthie nodded. "That makes sense. Magics, all magics, come at a cost. Apparently, even for charmlings."

"Really? Hold on." I raised an index finger to stop her. She wasn't going to distract me again. "I just accused you of murder. We need to stay on the topic at hand. Have you murdered anyone? Yes or no?"

"Pfft." She smoothed a lock of hair behind her ear. "Murder is such an ugly word."

"Grandma, did you kill a man?"

"Of course. I've killed three men, including your grandfather, Percy, but that was kind of his own fault."

EIGHT

*Karma's just sharpening her nails
and finishing her drink.
She'll be with you shortly.*
-Meme

My jaw hung off its hinges as I sat gaping at my grand-mother for a solid sixty seconds. My mind was trying to wrap itself around this new information: Ruthie Goode was a murderer.

"You murdered my grandfather and then named the house after him?"

She snorted. "Of course not. Technically, the house isn't named Percival. The man haunting it is. But over the years, he just sort of *became* the house." She spread her hands and looked around as though she were right there with us.

"Why is my grandfather haunting the house?"

"Because I killed him here, dear. Do try to keep up. He's buried in the backyard. It's okay, though. He hardly ever resurfaces. If he does, you can rent a backhoe from Kevin at North Shore Pizza and Equipment Rentals."

I scooted my chair back and gaped at her some more. Then at Roane. Apparently, that was my thing. "Did you know about this?"

"Defiance," she said, her tone admonishing. "That's very rude."

"Roane?"

He lifted a shoulder. "Like I said, nothing your grandmother does surprises me. I will say this, though. If she killed three men, they deserved it." He winked at Ruthie then stood and walked out without so much as a by-your-leave. Not that he needed my permission.

"Ruthie, I don't know what to think."

"I do." She beamed at me, her pretty face full of pride. "You, my dear, are ready. If you can hack my book of shadows, you are ready. You must get that protection spell up."

"First, I only hacked a couple of lines. Second, can we discuss the fact that you've taken not one, not two, but three lives?"

"Must we, darling? We need to get that spell—"

"—up. I get it. But why?"

"You're vulnerable."

"No, I mean, why did you kill three men?"

"You do realize that you fit your namesake to a tee."

I crossed my arms over the girls. "The deaths."

She sat down on what I assumed was a cloud, because what else would she sit on in the veil, and filled her lungs. "First you have to make me a promise."

"Fine."

"Dephne, a promise in our world is as good as a blood oath. You must keep it."

"Okay, what's the promise and I'll tell you for certain one way or the other."

"You must promise that if I tell you about the deaths, you will then raise the protection spell. Or die trying. No more questions. No more stalling."

I hadn't been stalling. Nevertheless, I agreed with a solemn nod.

"I'll start with the most recent."

Wait, die trying?

"The third man I killed was named Andrew Stemple. He was well on his way to becoming the most famous man in Massachusetts history. He was the next John Wayne Gacy."

I left it alone. "He was a serial killer?"

"We aren't certain he had reached the minimum kill requirement for that designation. Either way, if he hadn't, he was getting there. We do know that he killed at least two children. The police were looking into him when a good friend's daughter went missing."

"Oh, Grandma," I said. "I'm sorry."

"They came straight to me. I did a spell, but I'm not like you, dear girl. I have only traditional magics. They are nowhere near what you are capable of, so I couldn't narrow a location down enough for the mob—"

"The mafia was involved?"

"No. A group of citizens out for blood. By the time I'd finished the spell, they'd gathered at my door. All anger and hellfire. I knew if I sent them to the scour the area, they could tip Andrew off and he could kill the girl before they got to him."

I leaned in, completely absorbed. "What did you do?"

"We, actually. I sent the men to a warehouse that, while

close, I knew was not the actual location of Andrew's hide-out. Then I called an old friend who was on the force."

"The police force?" I asked, surprised.

She nodded. "He picked me up and we searched the backyards for the storage shed I'd caught a glimpse of in my vision. I was so panicked by that point. I knew the girl was still alive, but I also knew she wouldn't be for much longer."

"I can't imagine what that felt like."

"I hope you never have to."

"Wait. On the force? He wouldn't happen to be a tall wide-shouldered black man with sparkling eyes and a killer smile?"

"Maybe."

"You dragged Chief Metcalf into this?"

She deadpanned me. "He wasn't the chief yet, and he knew what he was getting into when he signed up to be my friend. May I continue?"

"Yes. Sorry."

"In the meantime, the mob realized I'd sent them to the wrong place and went back to the house. When they found me gone, they were not happy, but if they'd scared Andrew, he would have killed her instantly. I could see how unstable he was."

"What happened?"

She raised her brows as the memories flooded her mind. "I finally saw the storage shed. Houston parked the car and we made a plan. He went in through the front and I climbed in through a window in the back."

"He didn't call for backup?"

"We couldn't risk it. But, of course, Andrew heard me. It was a small window and I wasn't exactly known for my prowess."

My hands drifted up to cover my mouth.

"He took the girl hostage. Held a gun to her head as I stood there, helpless. Houston came up from behind and knocked him unconscious and I ran to the girl. Houston picked her up and I hugged them, then Andrew came to. Or he'd faked being unconscious. Either way, when I opened my eyes, he was standing behind Houston, gun pointed at his head, already pulling the trigger."

"Oh, no."

"It was instinct, really. I pushed every ounce of magic I had at him. Every molecule of energy. I watched as his head twisted on his body." She sat there for a long moment, lost in the past.

"Grandma?"

"The snap is what I remember most. His neck breaking. It was so loud."

I wished I could reach into the veil and hug her. "That's not murder. I mean—" I shook my head "—you saved that girl's life."

"He was so odd. His whole life, an outsider. I thought it sad until that night. He looked like Steve Buscemi only not as handsome."

That made me smile. "What did the mob do?"

She lowered her head. "Houston lied for me. Told the girl's parents he'd fought him and broke his neck during the altercation."

"When did this happen?"

She snapped back to the present and shrugged. "About five years after Percy passed."

"Was he your second? Percival?"

She shook her head. "The second involved an intruder and my double barrel Smith and Wesson."

"That'll do it. Is that the one you were accused of murder for?"

"No." She lowered her head again, and I was beginning to feel guilty about forcing her to tell me these stories. Forcing her to drudge up the past, memories she clearly wanted to stay buried.

Not guilty enough to stop her, apparently.

"No. That man had been breaking and entering houses all over town. He even put an elderly woman in the hospital when she caught him and, for reasons unknown, tried to stop him with a fly swatter. I decided not to try." She leveled an austere expression on me. "I decided to do."

God, my grandmother was a badass. "You're like Yoda, but that's still not murder."

"I guess not."

"One more, then," I said. "My grandfather." I stood to refresh my coffee and grab another slice of bacon.

"Yes, your grandfather."

Sitting down again, I asked, "Was this before I was born or after?"

"Before. Long before."

A soft shudder echoed through the house. I looked around.

"Is he there?" she asked me.

"I think so. Does he not want us talking about him?"

"Probably not, but it's not up to him."

Another shudder shook the ground, this one softer.

"I don't think he's too upset."

"It wouldn't matter either way," she said, glancing past me as though talking directly to her late husband. "It was your own fault."

No reaction that time.

"What happened?"

"First love," she said, a whimsical smile on her face.

"You know how we girls seem to be most attracted to the worst life has to offer? The rebellious ones?"

"The ones with a dark side?" I asked with a laugh. "I wouldn't know anything about that." Though that certainly described my ex to a tee. And I'd been more than old enough to know better.

"Exactly. That was Percy. Don't let his name fool you. He was a bad boy even in the witch world."

She had me practically drooling for more. "He was a witch, too?" I asked, surprised.

"He was. Unfortunately, he liked to experiment with darker magics. The stuff most witches steer clear of."

I sat with a half-eaten slice of bacon hovering near my mouth. "Black magic? That's a real thing?"

"It is."

"I thought it was just a song. What happened?"

"Like many before him, he went too far. Sank too deep. Got mixed up with some unsavory types and they tried things they should never have tried."

"Tried what?" I couldn't even begin to imagine.

She dipped her head and bit her lower lip. "Resurrection."

"From the dead?" I practically screeched the question, then I winced. That was loud. Still, resurrection?

"Once that dark magic gets a hold of you . . . It became an addiction, and he couldn't stop, until one day, something he brought back killed his best friend."

I stilled. Annette was going to kill me for letting her miss this. "Something . . . something he brought back?"

"It sliced through him like butter. He'd been mauled to death. Deep gashes all over his body."

I scooted back from the table in horror. "What the hell did he bring back? A werewolf?"

"I honestly don't know. He said he took care of it. It didn't matter at that point. I gave him an ultimatum. The magic or me."

"Oh, yeah. Willow went through that."

"He chose the magic." Her eyes glistened, but she raised her chin with her signature grace.

"I'm sorry, Grandma." She looked at me in surprise, though I couldn't imagine why. "Is that why you killed him?"

"No. Heavens no. We never use our magics for revenge. Karma is a real thing, Defiance."

The nod I gave her bordered on frenetic it was so vigorous. I raised my bacon. "Big believer."

"I didn't see him for two years after that. Your mother was twelve when he next showed up on our doorstep. He was a mess. Full of so much darkness. So much . . . well, evil. He couldn't shake it and he wanted to die but it wouldn't let him do it himself."

"I'm sorry, what?"

"The black magic. It wouldn't let him take his own life."

"It . . . it can control you?"

"The dark magics can, yes. That's why we don't mess with them unless we have absolutely no other choice."

"What happened? You took his life for him?"

"I did. I begged him to let me try to purify him, but he refused. He told me something I will never, ever forget. And I don't want you to forget it either, Defiance."

"Okay." I held my breath.

"He told me he would rather die than live without it."

"It really is like a drug."

"A powerful one. It was eating him alive but he would rather have died than live without the thing inside him."

"I'm sorry, Grandma How did you . . . how did he . . .?"

"It took my entire coven, actually.

"Covens are real?"

"As a heart attack. We had to trap him in a ritual circle and burn him with a kind of magical fire. It was a slow and agonizing death." Her hand shot to her mouth, the memory breaking her heart.

"I'm so sorry. I'll shut up now. We can do the spell thing. Or, you know, die trying."

"Thank you," she said.

"Oh, wait."

"Defiance."

"Real quick, was his death the one that got you accused of murder?"

"Yes. But it's difficult to prove a case of witchcraft these days. Not that the DA wasn't determined. He just had no evidence. And no body."

"Do you have a picture? I didn't see any of him on the walls."

Her walls were covered in old pictures of women going back several generations. No men. I hadn't even wondered why until now.

"In the hutch. The drawer on the left."

I hurried and took out a framed picture of a man that would've given Lucifer Morningstar a run for his money. The picture was from the tragic fashion era of the seventies, yet he didn't just pull it off, he owned it. He had a certain machismo. A *je ne sais quoi*. Inky black hair. Startlingly blue eyes. A face so perfect

I brought it back with me. "Holy crap, Ruthie. I can see the appeal."

She laughed softly and the house vibrated with warmth. He was such an eavesdropper.

"You look just like him," she said.

My gaze darted up. "In my dreams."

"You certainly didn't get your looks from me." She flipped the ends of her blond hair.

"Who did my mother look like?"

"Him. Always him." She said it so lovingly, I wanted to ask her how my mother died, but I'd made a promise. That story would have to wait.

"So, my grandfather just stuck around and became the house?"

"He did. And, by the way, dear, he's not really buried in the backyard."

"Oh, thank God." A wave of relief flooded every cell in my body.

"He's buried in the basement."

Cancel that. I bit back a shudder of revulsion. "A place I shall never see, then."

"Oh, trust me, you want to see the basement."

"Nope."

"You do."

"Never."

"Trust me."

"You couldn't get me down there with a taser and a stick of dynamite." No idea what that meant. I picked up my cup and stopped shaking my head long enough to take a sip.

"Roane lives there."

I spat coffee all over her face—a.k.a., my laptop—then proceeded to cough for the next five minutes.

"Trying your hand at swallowing, again?" Annette strolled in like she owned the place. "Practice makes perfect."

She poured a cup while waiting for me to finish convulsing.

I glared at Ruthie. "He's been living in this house without my knowledge? Aren't there are laws against that?"

"You made breakfast?" Nette asked.

I bit down and decided to take revenge on the woman who bore the woman who bore me. "My grandmother has killed three men."

Annette pressed her lips together, clearly impressed. "That's badass, Mrs. G."

I rolled my eyes so far back into my head I worried they'd get stuck that way, like my dads had warned me about all those years ago. I couldn't see anything in that state. Then another thought hit me.

"Wait, Roane lives in the basement with my departed grandfather's body?"

That got Annette's attention. "What?"

"Yes," Ruthie said. "Well, no. Not really. Only his bones."

"Roane lives in the basement?"

"The spell we used to kill him seared the flesh right off them. It was quite distressing. All I had to bury was his skeleton."

"The basement that sits directly below us?"

"Which made things much easier. You cannot imagine how much a hundred-seventy-pound body weighs."

"A hundred seventy pounds?" I guessed. Then I envisioned her dragging a body into the basement. "Grandma, that is the most disturbing thing you've said all morning."

A smile spread across her face.

"What?" I asked her, frustrated. "You keep smiling at me like that. This is not a smiling matter."

"You keep calling me Grandma."

"Do I?"

She beamed at me for a solid three seconds before

saying admonishingly, "Don't ever do that again. I'm Gigi. Short for Grammy Goode. It's what you called me when you were little."

"Gigi. I like it." Gigi, I could handle. Grammy Goode? Not so much.

"Can I call you Gigi?" Annette asked from over my shoulder.

The woman smiled. "If I can call you Nan."

"Mrs. Goode it is." She turned her attention to me. "Did you eat the last piece of bacon?"

"Gigi," I said, trying it on for size, "do you know what happened to Roane when he was a kid? Parris said something about his having a tragic past."

"I do, but it's not for me to say."

I had a feeling she'd take the high road. Freaking morals.

"I will tell you that he didn't talk because of it until he was seven years old."

"Seven?" I asked, a little heartbroken. What could've happened to him to cause such a lapse in development? Or, more likely, such an emotional barrier.

It made me want to get to know him even more. Like the kilt hadn't done that already.

NINE

I was taught to think before I act.
So if I smack you, rest assured,
I've thought about it
and am confident in my decision.
-T-shirt

Gigi. I'd have to get used to that one. It felt right, though. Like I did indeed have someone in my life named Gigi at some point. It was probably her.

After an hour straight of failed attempts at the protection spell, Ruthie thought that maybe taking a shower and putting on something other than Frozen pajamas might help relax me. I did feel like my nerves resembled my hair after Annette had given me a perm in high school: frazzled and crunchy.

The shower felt amazing. Not quite as amazing as when Roane helped me, but amazing nonetheless. I pulled back my impossibly thick, black hair, which was a bit on the nose for witchhood, and powdered my pale skin, making it look even paler. Dory Markham in high school used to call me a vampire. She wasn't too far off the mark, apparently.

After throwing on my last clean pair of jeans, a tan sweater, and brown suede boots, I headed down to try to protect myself from evildoers.

Turned out, however, there was one little thing wrong with the protection spell Gigi wanted me to do. She didn't know what it looked like. Not exactly, though she did have a couple of educated guesses.

"You don't know?" she asked me after our first several failed attempts. Panic raised her voice an octave.

"No. I thought you knew." I began panicking, too.

"I don't know the language. I told you. It's almost impossible to get any information. Charmlings are very well protected."

"At least they know the spell."

"You know it," Gigi said, pacing back and forth. "Let's think about this." She stopped and assessed me. "Are you concentrating?"

"Of course. Just in case, tell me what to concentrate on again."

She nodded in thought. "Okay, think about the fact that if you don't get this spell up, there are witches out there who will come, suck the life out of you, and take your power for themselves."

"They sound like my ex. Isn't there some kind of authority to prevent such things? Some type of magical law enforcement?"

"Like a council that governs our every move?"

"Exactly."

"No. There are for certain covens, but not for the witching world overall."

"Well, I think that's a terrible oversight. Someone needs to have our backs."

"Or try to control us."

"True. I guess."

"There are powerful covens who take it upon themselves to govern here and there. For the most part, however, we're on our own."

"And you're part of a coven, right?"

Her chin rose. "I am. You'll meet them soon. They're looking forward to it. Actually, some of them are downright giddy. Don't be surprised if you acquire some serious fans. You have quite the fanbase."

"How is that possible?"

"Because of me, partially, but mostly because of all you accomplished as a child."

I stopped waving my arm like an idiot and turned back to her. "What I accomplished as a child? What do you mean? What did I accomplish as a child?"

"That is for another time. Protection spell."

"Put your back into it," Annette said, then she giggled when I glared at her.

"After yesterday, I thought I'd have this down."

"You do. You tapped into your source. Now you just need to access the language. To learn how to bend it to your will."

"If I can't, I won't be any good to anyone."

"How did you read my book of shadows?"

"It just came to me. I thought about what I wanted to do, and the spell just popped into my head."

"Exactly. It's in there. Do that."

"I've been doing that."

"Well, do it again."

"Put your back into it," Annette repeated. She had raided Ruthie's library and was reading a volume on herbs and their different uses in the witch realm.

Fortunately for me, she took time out of her busy schedule to toss me advice every so often. No idea where I'd be without her. Probably better off, but would life be as fun? I didn't think so.

"Do it again." I shook it off. All of it. My failures. My expectations. My poor eating habits. I shook it all off, danced from foot to foot, rolled my head on my shoulders. I could do this. As soon as I answered the door.

A knock sounded right in the middle of my homage to Rocky.

"Defiance," Ruthie said. "Get back here."

"No can do, Gigi! My audience awaits. Or the mailman. Either way."

Fingers crossed this was not another loser. Of things. Loser of things. I was all booked up with zero talent to do anything about it. If anyone else needed something found, they'd just have to come back in my next life. Maybe I'd have my shit together by then. Doubtful, but I liked to think positive.

I opened the door and, honestly, if Mahatma Gandhi were standing there, I would've been less surprised.

"Kyle?" I asked, staring at my own reflection in my ex's shades.

His mother stood right beside him, craning her neck to get a better look at Percival. I felt dirty for him.

"What are you doing here?" Better yet, how did they find me? Why would they even want to?

He pushed past me to come inside. His mother followed.

"Come in," I said before closing the door.

Annette came to see who it was and stopped short. Her face flushed and her curls seemed to vibrate with anger.

"Annette," I said, my tone warning.

She spoke through clenched teeth. "What the hell are they doing here?"

"Go back to the kitchen and keep Gigi company." I had no clue why my ex and his Machiavellian mother would be here, but I didn't need Annette escalating what promised to be an already explosive situation, especially since her nickname in high school was Nitro. As in nitroglycerin. As in unstable AF.

Erina perched her taut ass on the edge of the wingback, crinkling her nose at the décor. "It's a little dank, don't you think?"

"Your face is a little dank," Annette said.

"Annette, it's okay. You can go back to the kitchen."

She looked me up and down and said softly so only I could hear, "There is only one way I'm leaving you alone with them, and unless you suddenly figure out how to wield that magic productively, that ain't happening."

She strode in, tore a sheet off another chair, and plopped down in it.

Kyle sat on the couch and since I wasn't about to sit next to him, I remained standing. "What do you want?"

He spread his hands and glanced around, indicating Percy. What the actual fuck? He already took everything. How did he think for a moment he'd end up with Percy, too? And why did he even want him?

"You didn't declare this during the divorce proceedings," he said.

"I didn't have this during the divorce proceedings."

"Oh, please," Erina said.

Erina Julson was a mixture of gentle breeding and the belly of a snake. The part that slithers across the hot desert sand. She had perfectly coiffed mahogany hair with eyes to match. While Gigi was the picture of elegance and grace, Erina was a facsimile. A wannabe. A low-quality photocopy. I never realized how much so until now.

"You had to know you were coming into this property. I find it very suspicious that hardly a month has gone by since the divorce and you just magically end up with a property worth a fortune."

She had no idea how magical it was. "I had no clue I was going to get this," I said, not that it mattered. She would never believe me. I could tell her orange juice came from oranges and she'd call me a liar. To my face. While hers bore a sinister smile.

Annette chimed in. Again. Unwantedly. "I find it very suspicious that your anti-aging cream is doing such a poor job. You should look into that."

"Dee," Kyle said, holding his arms out helplessly. "Can we talk without your guard dog present?"

Wrong thing to say. "Only if we can talk without your babysitter present."

Erina's gaze snapped to me, daggers shooting from her eyes. I never really understood that metaphor until now. I liked it.

"Kyle, I'm busy. What the hell are you doing here? You already have everything."

Erina rolled her eyes. "It was all in my name. It's not like we stole it from you."

"Wow," I said, sitting at last. I took the opposite end of

the sofa. The farthest spot I could manage. "You almost sound like you believe that. You're a much better actress than I've given you credit for."

"Dee, we didn't come here to fight."

"Why did you come here, *Kay*?"

He pressed his mouth together at my use of his most hated nickname. "We came to make a deal."

My suspicion skyrocketed. "What else could you possibly want from me?"

"This house."

They weren't kidding. "You're not kidding." I was so stunned, the edges of my vision blurred.

"Not at all," Erina said.

Annette snorted. By far her best sound effect. "And what makes you think you have a snowball's chance of taking it from her?"

"You misunderstand" Kyle's voice was soft. Appeasing. I'd learned to distrust this side of him months ago. "We want to make a trade."

This was getting good. "What kind of trade?"

"The restaurant for the house."

Surprise shot through me. Why would they trade my restaurant for this house? Unless . . . "You're running my restaurant into the ground already?"

"Dee, calm down. We're doing no such thing. We just want to make a move and this is the perfect place to do it."

My mind raced trying to figure out why they would want this house. True, it was probably worth more than my restaurant, but I felt like there was more to it than that. "What do you know that I don't?"

"What? Nothing. You've always been so suspicious."

"I can't imagine why," Annette said.

"Tell her, Kyle," Erina snapped. "Or I will."

"Mother." He drew in a deep breath, and sickening sense of dread crept up my spine. "Make the trade, Dee, and we won't take you back to court."

I had to admit. I wasn't expecting that. "On what grounds?"

"On withholding the value of your assets. You didn't declare this property."

"I just signed the papers on it three days ago!" I jumped to my feet. "I didn't even know about it. I didn't even know I had a grandmother."

He stood as well. "And you can have your lawyer tell that to the judge."

They knew I couldn't afford a lawyer. They were counting on it. But my mind was stuck in a groove, replaying the same question over and over. Why would they want this house? Why would they come all the way from Arizona to try to get it? And how had they even found out about it?

I had to admit, getting my restaurant back would be a dream come true. It wasn't like I could afford Percy anyway.

"Look," he said, the snake scales he'd inherited from his mother glistening in the morning sun as he leaned closer, "we don't have to do this. We can make a trade. Even swap. Right here and now."

A male voice interrupted my thought process, which was already a bit frazzled. "There you are," Roane said, walking into the room.

We turned and watched him walk in. He was breathtaking. His hair mussed like he'd just woken up. His lashes dark with sleep.

Annette's sharp intake of breath told me that she noticed, too.

But he didn't stop. He kept walking, like a predator stalking his prey, until we stood toe-to-toe. Then, without hesitation, he wrapped a hand around the back of my head, bent and planted his mouth on mine.

The kiss started out slow. What I thought was going to be a simple peck morphed into an all-out mack session when he tilted his head and pushed his tongue past my lips.

I grabbed hold of his T-shirt for balance and his other hand slid to the small of my back, his fingers splayed. Within seconds, he deepened the kiss. A surge of pleasure laced up my skin and dipped low in my abdomen. His mouth was hot and wet and pliant. All the things I was.

Then, as quickly as it began, it ended. He broke it off and smiled down at me. "I thought we could do lunch at Finz when you're hungry."

I barely managed a nod.

His olive eyes were full of amusement when he wrapped a possessive arm around me and faced our company. "Who are your friends?"

"They—" I stopped and cleared my throat. "They were just leaving."

"Good."

Kyle's face had turned a rather hilarious shade of magenta, as did Erina's. Before he could say anything else, the front door opened.

Chief Metcalf walked in, shook out his jacket—apparently it was raining—and waved a big hello.

"Oh, hey, Roane," he said, a bright smile on his face. "Hey, daffodil."

"Chief."

He gave Erina and Kyle a once-over then said to me, "I guess you forgot to mention the restraining order to these fine folks."

I blinked in confusion. "Restraining order?"

"You're going to get these two arrested if you aren't careful. To be honest, I don't want either one of them sullying up my jail."

"Arrested?" Erina asked, her bright complexion picking up the lovely pinks in her fluffy coat like she'd matched them on purpose.

"I have a court order." He slid a folded paper out of his inside pocket. When he showed it to them, his demeanor changed. He grew serious, his large frame even more intimidating than it had been five seconds earlier. "If either of you set foot in this town again, I'll arrest you so fast your lawyer's head will spin."

"That's not possible," Kyle said. "You can order us from an entire town."

"It is, actually. Judge Brigalow? Big fan of our girl here." He nodded toward me. "So, you can take it up with her, but I'd hurry. You have fifteen minutes to get out before I send for a patrol car."

"This isn't over," Erina said, gathering her bag and storming toward the door.

"That's exactly what it is," the chief said, an edge to his voice so sharp it could've sliced through cold metal.

I fell a little in love, truth be known.

He stepped closer, towering over the woman to punctuate his next point. "If you even think about dragging Ms. Dayne into court again for any reason whatsoever, you will live to regret it."

"And just how would you manage that from Massachusetts?"

"Did I mention I'm very good friends with both the police commissioner in Phoenix and the health inspector?

Speaking of which," he glanced at his watch, "your restaurant is getting a surprise visit in about thirty minutes."

Kyle gaped at me, clearly taken off guard.

"That was beautiful," Annette said, but she had yet to take her eyes off Roane.

Without another word, they left. Erina was appalled. Kyle, on the other hand, had turned an interesting shade of green. Not his best color. I didn't think he had enough brains to know when to back down. I was glad to see I was wrong.

Then again, he glanced over his shoulder at me and the look in his eyes, the dangerous glint . . . I'd never seen that in him before.

"Thank you," I said to the chief when they left. "I didn't know cops could lie like that."

"Firstly, we can. Secondly, I wasn't lying." He offered me the paper. "This is a real court order."

I tore it out of his hands and began reading. He wasn't kidding. "How?"

"Thank your grandmother. Oh, and the judge of course. She really is a big fan."

"She doesn't even know me."

Roane spoke up then. "When are you going to learn, beautiful, everyone knows you here. You're practically a celebrity."

No pressure then. "Why?"

"You'll figure it out," he said, a mischievous twinkle in his eye.

"I'm off to do cop stuff," the chief said. "Tell your grandmother hi for me."

"Will do. Thank you so much, Chief."

He waved as he walked out. I waved back then turned to Roane. "I owe you again."

He dropped his arm and put some distance between us. "You owe me nothing."

I stepped back, too, not wanting to crowd him. "Also, you live in the basement."

"She told you?"

"Why didn't you?"

"I don't know. When I moved in, it wasn't my finest hour. I didn't want you to think I was taking advantage of your grandmother."

"From what little I know about my grandmother, she was the one doing the taking. My point was, you live in the basement. The one with Percy's bones buried in it."

A deep laugh escaped him, like cool water on a hot day. "It's not like I keep them on an altar."

I tried to suppress a frown. In true Defiance fashion, I failed. God forbid I break the failing streak I was on. "It doesn't bother you?"

"Living in a basement? Not really."

That time I laughed. "Living with Percy's bones."

He ducked his head, and said softly, "I've lived with far worse."

At that exact moment, as though we were in perfect sync, as if our hearts beat as one, as if the stars had aligned just for us, we remembered we had company. We turned our heads to the curly-headed imp standing close beside us. Like really close. Lids round. Jaw slack.

"Annette," I said in acknowledgment.

"I've never seen anyone with such exquisite coloring."

Roane gave me a quick once over. "Neither have I."

"I'm pretty sure she was referring to you."

She reached up and fondled a strand of his golden-streaked red hair. "Is this your real color? Please tell me it's your real color."

"She really does have manners," I said to him.

She recovered, dropped his hair, and gave the poor guy some space. "Sorry. I don't normally assault people when I first encounter them. At the very least, I usually wait until our third." She started backing away. "I'm just going to, you know, go die." Then, with shoulders hunched, she hurried away.

"Sorry about that." I pointed in her general direction. "She's a hoot. For real, though, is that your natural color?"

"Depends." He grew serious, his eyes glistening as he took me in, his gaze a powerful mix of curiosity and, dare I hope, desire.

My heartbeats faltered, stumbling into one another as I struggled for air.

"Do you like it?"

I confirmed with a slow nod. "I like it."

"Then yes."

A soft bubble of laughter fought its way to the surface. "That cleared up nothing, just so you know."

He lifted a shoulder, completely unapologetic.

"And if I didn't like it?"

"It would still be my natural color."

"Good to know."

He inched closer, his alluring scent tempting me to do the same. He was going to kiss me again. I could feel it. I wanted it more than anything else on earth at that moment in time, if not for the brash voice of Annette yelling at me from the top of her lungs.

"Deph! Your grandmother says to stop dillydallying and get your ass back to work! Also, I'm paraphrasing."

He lowered his head. "I better get back to work, too."

"Oh. Right. Okay."

He walked away. I watched him walk away. I may have

drooled. I finally knew what the saying *sex on a stick* meant. All in all, this whole adventure had proven very educational on several levels.

About thirty seconds after he disappeared, Ink barreled toward me like his tail had caught fire. He stopped to rub my ankles suggestively and didn't get too upset when I picked him up and took him to the kitchen with me.

After plopping down in my regular chair, I buried my face in his fur and said to Ruthie, "I don't know where you found that man, but we need to invest in stock. They make good stuff."

"I concur," Annette said. "Really, really good stuff. Excellent quality."

"Yes, they do. Now—"

"Are there such things as shapeshifters?"

"You're stalling again."

"No, I'm not. It's just, you said Roane lives in the basement. Ink lives in the basement. I've never seen them at the same time. I just thought, you know, shapeshifter."

"How cool would that be?" Annette asked from behind her book.

"Well, I can tell you that Ink and Roane are not the same being. Now concentrate."

"Gigi, I have been concentrating. Maybe we need to try a different tact."

"I thought it was tack," Annette said.

"How about we try this?"

"Or is it *change tack*?"

"Think about all the ways you're going to lose this house to those vultures if they decide to take you to court," Ruthie said. "That should get you angry. You know, light a fire under your settee, as it were."

I rubbed Ink's nose. He did *not* appreciate it. "You heard that?"

Her expression hardened. "Honestly, what were your fathers thinking?"

"They had nothing to do with it, Gigi. I'm a big girl. I made my bed. I'll probably lose Percy anyway, so it really doesn't matter."

He delicate brows slid together. "What do you mean?"

"Gigi," I said, setting Ink free. He scampered off to do cat stuff. "I'm sorry to have to tell you this, but I don't think I can keep him."

"Ink?"

"Percy."

"What?" she asked, stunned.

"I can't afford him."

"What's there to afford, sweetheart?"

"Well, for starters, insurance? Taxes? Utilities? General upkeep? The neighbors are already threatening to tear him down."

She crossed her arms. "They couldn't do that even if they wanted to. How about we cross that bridge when we come to it. You may not believe me right now, but how you are going to keep Percival is the least of your worries."

"Right. Evil witches en route."

"Exactly."

"Dark sorcerers incoming."

"Yes."

"Black mages approach."

"Defiance."

"Okay." I slumped in the chair.

"Up," she ordered. Sassy thing.

After rolling onto my feet with a few groans thrown in for good measure, I turned the laptop to face the kitchen. I was beginning to wonder how a kitchen became our secret lair when I remembered where the coffee pot lived.

"I'm not going to coach you this time. You can do it. You have it in you."

"I can do it. Right." But how? That was still the question.

"I want you to know," she added, "if they do come, if a witch powerful enough to steal your life energy makes it past the front door, you will not be the only casualty."

I whirled around to her. "What do you mean?"

Annette lowered the book and listened in as well.

"I mean, who do you think will try to protect you?"

My thoughts stalled.

"Who do you think will *die* trying to protect you?"

I looked at Annette, whose expression resembled mine. Wary and ready to rabbit.

"Yes," Ruthie said, her affirmation turning my stomach. "And who else?"

No. "Roane?"

"Of course."

"No. He just . . . we just met. Why would he—"

"And who else?"

I shook my head. "I don't know."

"Percival may have lost himself in dark magics, but he still loves you, Defiance. You're still his granddaughter."

"No. He can't be killed."

"He can be . . . disassociated."

"What does that mean?"

"He can be uncoupled from this realm. He can cease to exist on this plane. They can, essentially, send him to the underworld."

The walls hummed with a soft vibration, much like Ink's purr, fascinating and oddly comforting.

Annette put the book down and walked over to me. "We can do this, Deph. Concentrate, damn it."

The thought of losing her. Of losing any of them . . . "Wait. Gigi, what about you?"

Her face softened and a sad smile thinned her lips. "If they win, darling girl, they could never let me live, even in the veil."

TEN

People who tolerate me on a daily basis . . .
they're the real heroes.
-Meme

I sank into the chair, trying to absorb what Ruthie had just told me. Mainly the fact that people could die trying to protect me. That they could even get to her. "How could they get to you in the veil?"

"That's not what matters right now."

"Gigi, enough. How could they get to you?"

"There are, even in this realm, unsavory elements. I don't want you to think about that right now."

"How can I not?"

She raised her chin. "You're right. I apologize. I'm not trying to scare you, sweetheart. I just want you to know all the angles. All that's at stake. What could happen if we fail."

And I'd been joking about my streak.

"If I disappear, you must figure out the spell immediately. That's your only hope."

I leaned forward and touched her face on the screen. "Has something happened?"

"Nothing of note. But you must hurry."

Perhaps it was her expression. Perhaps it was the defiant tilt of her chin, or the thought of losing the ability—no, the honor—of seeing it ever again that did it. That final push of motivation that I'd so desperately needed.

I felt the magics stir within me. I felt them heat until a spark ignited and a flame took hold. I looked down at my torso. Splayed my fingers over my chest. Pulled the fire out until it was in the palm of my hand.

I didn't think of the word Ruthie had been wanting me to envision. It wouldn't have worked. Not for what she wanted. I needed a spell to diffuse the essence of my energy so no one, not even a powerful GPS, could find me.

I raised my hand and drew the symbol for a spell that basically meant to scatter. To dissipate. To disappear.

Just as before, light bled from the lines I drew, golden and bright, as though the sun itself were leaking out of them. Sharp edges. Swirling loops. I drew it again and again as I turned to complete the circle. To disperse my energy. To disguise it.

The pain was even less than the second time I'd used the magics, but something else happened as well. The more I drew, the more I kept the magics flowing through me, the more knowledge I acquired. A script came to me. A chant. I felt the original witches. I felt their fears and frustrations. Their hopes and deepest dreams.

They wanted their daughters to live unafraid of persecution, so they created the sources, the charmlings, to strike a balance in both the magic and the non-magic worlds.

Back then, they were not called witches or shrews or crones. This was long before such derogatory terms for the gifted. It was a time when witches were seen as shamans. Healers. Alchemists. They were the highest-ranking priest-esses and were called, in rough translation, the charmed. Yet even then, there were those who would take advantage. Those who would destroy.

Thus, the original charmed created their queens, the charmlings. Three beings of great power to maintain balance and keep their sisters safe.

These charmlings were meant to live apart from both the mundane and the witch worlds. To separate themselves and watch from afar. To help when they could. At the same time, they were meant to live together. To work side-by-side with their sisters. To pool their magics and govern the world as one.

Sadly, centuries later, dark forces figured out how to kill them and commandeer their powers. They sought them out. Separated them. Murdered them one by one and stole their energy. As strong as the charmlings were, they trusted too much. They were unworldly and didn't know the true meaning of evil.

When a charmling was killed and a witch tried to steal her powers, if a child was born anywhere on earth with the blood of the original charmed, that child would inherit the power. She would steal it away from the witch trying to take it.

But those who were born a charmling, unless they were born to a very knowledgeable family who could cast the spells to protect them immediately, were quickly snatched up by dark mages, killed and their powers siphoned away.

Still, a witch who killed and took a charmling's power risked almost certain death. Because others would come.

Maybe not today, maybe not tomorrow, but eventually another witch would try to take what was never rightfully hers in the first place.

Those who did manage to hold onto the power were usually protected by a dark coven who used the magics for their own gain. They were essentially chattel. Very well-guarded and treated like royalty, but they had a startling lack of free will. Thus, either road led to tragedy.

I saw a face in the mists of time. Just for a second before it disappeared. Large dark eyes. Ebony skin. Bright paints. I whirled around, trying to find it again. Trying to find her. I searched over and over through the light I'd created and the darkness beyond. The smoke whirled around me. Nothing for minutes and then another face. And another.

Each face, stunning in the swirling vapors, painted with bright golds and reds and blues. Their inklike hair braided with shimmering golden threads.

The beauty in the middle raised her hand and drew a symbol. I knew it instantly: Of royal blood.

"Defiance?"

I heard Ruthie's voice but couldn't quite figure out which direction it was coming from.

I turned back to the charmed, lifted my hand and drew the symbol. They bowed their heads and then dissipated into the mist. The same mist that vanished seconds later when I found myself staring at the ceiling.

Annette stood over me, a cold washcloth in hand.

"Oh, good. I was about to slap you," she said.

I grabbed the cloth and sat up, trying to steady myself through a dizzying wave. "What the hell?"

"You face planted," Annette said.

I climbed onto a chair like I'd had twelve margaritas too

many—because that happened once—and looked at my grandmother.

"You did it," she said, clasping her hands in front of her. "You cast the spell. You're safe. For now."

"Am I going to pass out every time I do a spell?"

"I don't think so. I think this is just your body adjusting."

Annette agreed with a nod, already an expert.

"How long was I out?"

"Only a few minutes," Annette said. She was the worst liar ever.

I looked at the clock on my laptop. "I've been out for two hours?" I screeched. Then I felt a warmth on my cheek. "Annette, did you slap me?"

Guilt consumed her. She looked away, and said, "Only once."

"You just lied again!"

"Okay, twice. I panicked. You were out cold. I was about five seconds away from calling an ambulance when you woke up."

Then I remembered what happened. I stared at Ruthie, my mind officially blown. "The original witches, the charmed, they were from Mesopotamia."

"Well, yes, but . . . wait." She stepped closer. "Did you see them?"

"I did." I sat in front of her, blood rushing in my ears. "They were stunning. Powerful. Majestic."

She pressed her hands to her heart. "Good heavens. I've always dreamed of meeting them in the veil. Did they speak to you?"

"They wrote in the air."

Annette, impatient as ever, blurted out, "What did they say?"

I shrugged. "Simply, 'Of royal blood.'"

Ruthie's hands covered her mouth and she closed her eyes as though basking in the moment.

"Gigi, that was amazing and all, but it was just a hallucination, right? From the spell?" I knew the answer before she spoke. It just boggled my mind so much.

"No, darling girl. It was not a hallucination."

"What did you do?" Annette asked, her voice full of awe. "When they drew the symbol, what happened next?"

"I drew it back. It was almost like a greeting or a secret handshake. And they told me everything."

"The true history?" Ruthie said.

"Yes. You pretty much nailed it." I chewed on my bottom lip a few minutes, then said, "Ruthie, I don't know what you did, but you saved my life. I would never have lived to see my first birthday if not for you."

Her face softened and tears pooled between her lids. "I'm so honored, Defiance."

"I am, too," Annette said.

I stood and walked over to her. She made a cross with her index fingers and raised it to ward me off. Thankfully, that only worked on vampires. She tried to back away. I threw my arms around her anyway and pulled her into a hug.

"Still not a hugger," she said into my sweater. After a minute, she said in a high-pitched voice, "It burns."

I hugged her harder before a thought occurred to me. "Oh, my God. We have to find Mrs. Touma. The woman with Alzheimer's. Maybe I can do it, now."

"Of course you can, dear. I would like to suggest, however, that we start with something that has a little less potential for human casualty."

"You're right. The wedding ring?"

A pleased smile spread across her face. "The wedding ring."

I looked over at Annette. "You ready?"

"Let's do this."

We grabbed our coats and headed for the back door. Apparently, Dana Hart lived behind Percy, her house one street over on Warren.

"Wait. I stopped and turned back to Ruthie. How do I find things? Like, where do I make the symbol? What symbol do I make?"

"Well, I could tell you how I used to find lost items for people, but that would be like teaching an Olympic sprinter how to walk."

Honestly, the woman could be so cryptic. "Meaning?"

"You don't need to learn to walk when you can sprint at the speed of light. It will come to you. Just focus on what you want to accomplish."

Annette cocked her head to one side in thought. Never a good thing. "What about things she wants other people to accomplish? Like, say, she wants her bestie to accomplish a dozen donuts a day without weight gain. Is that doable?"

Ruthie offered her a patient grin.

"Okay, well, think about it and get back to me."

"Besides, you've done it before," Ruthie said.

We'd been heading out the door when she spoke. We turned back, and I offered her a dubious scowl. "Not without gaining weight. That's a lot of carbs, Gigi."

Another one of those patient grins.

"Okay, I'll bite. I've done what before? Found things?"

"Oh, honey, you've performed miracles."

I walked back to her. Or, well, to my laptop. "What kinds of miracles?"

"The miraculous kind."

I sat at the table again while Annette struggled with the zipper of her winter coat. We didn't wear them often in Phoenix. "That doesn't help."

"Remember the other files in this folder?"

"Oh, yeah, I forgot about those."

"Open the one titled Missing Child."

I stilled and sat there for a long moment, before asking, "I found a missing child?"

A knowing grin spread across her lovely face. "Open the file."

I went back to the folder. There were three files in it besides the one where Ruthie lived. Which was so weird. Sure enough, one was titled Missing child.

After a quick glance at Annette, who was standing behind me, I clicked on the mp4 file. A square screen popped up of a dimly lit room. It only took a second to realize it was Ruthie's living room. I could hear soft chanting and a woman crying in the background.

"Ruthie, what is this?"

She didn't answer. She didn't say anything.

The camera bounced in and out of focus. It panned out to show a circle of women holding hands around a map. They sat on the floor with candles flickering in front of them.

Then one woman leveled her hand over the map, fingers splayed, palm down as she circled her hand over it. The chanting grew louder and the woman's hand shook, and when the camera swung around, a younger version of Ruthie came into frame.

After a moment, she closed her hand into a fist and doubled over.

"I'm sorry," she said, her voice weak.

The crying grew louder. "Please," a woman said. She

was not in the frame, so I couldn't see who it was. It didn't matter. I could tell she was desperate. In pain. Her voice divulging the agony she felt. "Please try again."

Then, as though there was nothing unusual about the situation whatsoever, a woman holding a sleeping child, no older than three, walked into the room. She could barely be seen in the top corner of the frame as she carried the girl toward the circle.

The woman had thick, dark hair, much like tangled mop atop the girl who wore pink pajamas, and carried a stuffed cat. A stuffed cat I still had in my chest at home.

My pulse quickened.

The woman knelt down, her face dire, and gently woke the little girl.

"Defiance," she said softly. "Deph, honey, wake up." Was that my mother? I'd been here over two days and had yet to see a picture of her. I hadn't even asked to see one, and I wondered why.

"I don't think we should do this," Ruthie said.

"Please, Ruthie," the woman crying off-camera said. "I'll do anything." She broke down, her wailing heartbreaking.

I finally roused and immediately climbed into Ruthie's lap only to fall back asleep again almost instantly.

With a resigned sigh, Ruthie stroked my back. "Defiance, honey, can you wake up?"

After a moment of cajoling, I squirmed then lifted my lids and looked around as though realizing for the first time something was not right.

I rubbed my eyes and glanced up at Ruthie.

"Sweetheart, Mrs. Huber's son is missing. Can you find him?"

My head tilted to look past Ruthie and, I assumed, find Mrs. Huber. Then I nodded. I climbed out of Ruthie's lap and walked toward Mrs. Huber. A bundle of nerves, she appeared in the frame at last.

When I got to her, I took her hand, but just for a moment, then I turned to the map and, as though I did that sort of thing every day, I stood over the map and drew a symbol in the air, the spell for *reveal*.

The symbol glowed, and I did something I didn't know to do, yet. I physically pushed the spell onto the map. I opened my palm and forced the spell onto the parchment.

The second it touched the paper it began to disperse. Molecule by molecule it covered the map like a thick, searching fog, then slowly vaporized and disappeared.

"There," I said, pointing to a spot on the map, before climbing back onto Ruthies lap.

Two men shot forward to see where I'd pointed, as did Mrs. Huber, her actions frantic as she studied it. The men talked quietly. One was a younger version of Chief Metcalf. He glanced at Ruthie, graced Mrs. Huber with a reassuring nod, then took off with his partner.

"Is that it?" Mrs. Huber asked, shaking visibly. "Is she sure?"

"She's sure," Ruthie said, her tone understanding and firm at once. She stood with me in her arms and took me out of the room.

"You found him," Ruthie said when the video ended. "Houston got there and found him. They took down the boy's father who, if the shovel was any indication, was going to bury him that night."

"Why?" I asked, appalled.

"Custody battle gone awry."

Sometimes I thought I would never understand the human psyche. "He was okay? The boy?"

She nodded. "Thanks to you."

I sat astonished. "And I just knew?" I asked her. "I just knew how to do it?"

"Yes, dear. Like I said, you were born knowing the language. It was as natural to you as breathing is to us. And let me assure you, your gifts kept you in plenty of hot water."

"That was my mother?"

Her mouth thinned. "Yes."

I nodded. "She was so pretty. Like you."

"Thank you. She was." She played with a necklace at her throat. "She was beautiful."

"Wait," Annette said, her brows sliding together. She looked me up and down. "That was you in the video?"

"She's quick," Ruthie said.

"Like a fox." I filled my lungs and glanced at Annette. "Are you still up for this?"

"Dude, I was born up for this. Wouldn't miss it for the world."

I picked up my phone then had a thought. "Gigi, can I download your file-slash-app onto my phone and, you know, bring you along?"

A look of surprise adorned her lovely face. "I don't see why not. I mean, if I'm available, sure."

My expression flatlined. "Why wouldn't you be available?

"I do have other acquaintances, Defiance."

"Acquaintances?"

She cleared her throat, clearly uncomfortable. "I have a friend."

It was my turn to be surprised. "Really? You're talking to someone else?"

Annette's synapses chose that moment to fire faster than

mine. "Does that friend happen to be a tall, ruggedly handsome police chief?"

Ruthie blushed. The woman actually blushed. Without a drop of blood in her body, she blushed. Online dating in the afterlife just seemed wrong somehow.

"Grandma!"

ELEVEN

*I'm not sure if I attract crazy,
or if I make them that way.*
-T-shirt

Since Dana Hart, the missing wedding ring girl, had used our backdoor, we decided to use hers. It was easier than walking all the way around the block. The crisp air smelled like the ocean today, rich and briny. It made me want to hunt down a beach and build a campfire.

We entered through Dana's back gate.

"You still with me?" I asked Ruthie.

"I am, but you may not want to let Dana see me like this. Not just yet. It's a lot to take in."

"Amen to that." I locked my phone as Annette knocked on the door.

Dana opened it, her brows drawn in confusion.

Then I realized her husband could've come home early

and tried to cover. "Hi, Dana. Have you heard about our lord and savior—?"

"Come in!" She practically dragged us inside. "Did you find it?"

Poor thing was in a state of panic. Her messy bun was messier than most. She wore the same clothes she'd had on the day before. And her house had been torn apart. I could practically feel the stress seeping out of her, and it worried me.

Annette picked her way through the carnage to get at a pair of wiener dogs who'd clearly been traumatized by their mother's behavior.

I put a hand on her arm to get her attention. "Dana, are you in danger?"

"What?"

"If your husband comes home and you don't have the ring, will he harm you in any way?"

Her expression told me I'd caught her off guard. She quickly put me at ease, though. "What? No. No, that's not the problem." She dragged me into the living room. I tried to pet the dogs. Apparently, there was no time for that. My bad. "It's his mother. She'll never forgive me if I lose the family heirloom. Trust me when I say that woman can hold a grudge until the stars burn out."

"You know my mother-in-law?" I asked, feigning surprise.

She laughed. "Yours, too?"

"Don't get me started. Mine is actually an ex-mother-in-law, so I'm slowly regaining my will to live."

"The road to recovery can be a long one."

"Word."

We sat on a beige sofa in a room that was slightly less post-apocalyptic than what we'd seen so far and slightly more disaster movie of the week. So, not hit quite as hard by Hurricane Dana.

Annette was on the ground, playing with Dana's wieners. I wanted to play with her wieners. Instead, I put on my big-girl panties and behaved professionally. I had to do Ruthie proud.

"So, you figured it out?" Dana asked. "You know now?"

I chewed on my lower lip for a moment, then said, "I'm still in the process of figuring it out. I don't know if I can help you, Dana."

She balled her hands into fists in excitement, hope bursting out of her. "It's okay. I'm begging you to just try."

"I have to admit, I'm not sure what to do. What did my grandmother do when she helped you find something?"

"She did a spell. Very witchy with herbs and, I don't know, something that looked like dandelions pappus. You know, the fuzzy white things?"

"Right. Well, I don't know how to work with herbs yet."

"No, I know," she said, growing excited. "She said you wouldn't have to use herbs. She said you were different."

I loved that she told so many people. They seemed to know more about me than I did.

Annette came to sit with us. She took a chair catty-corner to me and I finally got to say hello to the dogs. They seemed as excited about that fact as I was. Then I took my cues from the video Ruthie showed me. I took Dana's hand into mine. She tried to rein in her elation by taking deep breaths and letting me work.

I noticed from my periphery Annette scooted to the edge of her seat in anticipation. Great. I'd let them both down if I couldn't pull this off.

"You should breathe," Annette said.

"I am breathing."

"No, like deep, soothing breaths. Let the energy flow through you." She wiggled her fingers over her body to demonstrate.

After tossing her a quick glare, I tried to focus.

"Sorry," she whispered. Like a whisper wouldn't be just as much of a distraction.

Having no idea what I was supposed to be focusing on, I decided to begin by just trying to calm down. To let my energy flatline before asking anything of it. My lids drifted shut and I focused on Dana's hand in mine. On her essence. I let our energies weave together and merge until I saw the thing in her mind that weighed the most. The ring.

It was a silver oval with a sprinkling of tiny diamonds. Strong, like the women who wore it, it only *looked* delicate. Also like the women who wore it.

Dana's sense of urgency flowed into me and spurred me into action. I stood, walked to the center of the room, and drew the spell in the air. The light bleeding from the lines cast a soft glow, like candlelight, on the objects around me.

The dogs barked, but I was lost. Nothing could break my concentration now. It was like the ring beckoned. Called out to me. Like it wanted to be found.

I opened my palm and pushed the spell to the floor. Forced it into a mist. Ordered it to reveal the ring's location. I must've sucked at giving orders, however, because it didn't reveal a single location. It revealed three.

I could see them in my mind's eye, like I was standing in front of each of them. One in the backyard. One in a bathroom. One a safety deposit box.

Confusion snapped me out of the spell. I turned to Dana, her expression so hopeful, it broke my heart.

Instead of trying to explain, I went in search of the bathroom. Annette and Dana bolted out of their chairs and followed. I unscrewed the stopper to the sink.

"I've already looked there," Dana said. "I even removed the trap, and took apart—"

She stopped when she watched me turn the stopper over. It was the kind that one only had to push down to close the drain. The ring had wedged itself inside the inner workings of the stopper. She probably would've figured it out if she'd tried to close the drain. The ring wouldn't have allowed it.

I pried the ring out and handed it to a woman who defined joy and gratitude and relief. Mostly relief.

She teared up and threw her arms around me. I hugged her back, then Annette decided to get in on the action and hugged us, too.

"Dana," I said, hating to be a buzzkill. "I'm not finished. There's more."

She wrenched back. "There's more?"

I nodded and hurried past them to get to the backyard. The dogs followed, nipping at my heels in excitement. Now that I knew they were here, I'd definitely have to come for a visit.

Exiting out the back door disoriented me. The vision from the spell looked different, but I quickly got my bearings and marched to a spot not far from the wrap-around porch. I knelt down and began to dig into the ice-cold ground. Dirt caked under my nails. It didn't matter. I had to get to it.

"Um, Defiance?" Dana asked, her voice hesitant.

"Just a sec."

Annette decided to give it a go. "So, D-bomb." She squatted down next to me, and asked in a sing-song voice, "Whatcha doin'?"

"Finding the ring."

"But you already found the ring," Dana said, confused.

I continued to dig. Thankfully the ground was wet, but that fact also made it colder. My sleeves, now damp around the wrists, were beginning to stiffen with the cold. My fingers cramped. Though my nails would never be the same, I continued to dig.

After a moment, Annette dropped to her knees to help. We dug for several minutes until she stopped and looked up at me, her mouth forming a pretty O.

She lifted her hand out of the hole we'd dug and brought with it another ring, this one exactly like the first one.

She handed the mud-covered heirloom to Dana, whose expression turned from wariness to confusion. Then it hit her. She looked at the ring on her finger. "You mean, this isn't the original ring?" Her gaze slid to mine. "This isn't the heirloom?"

"Oh, but wait," I said, sounding like a TV spokesperson. "There's more. There's a third ring. It's at Eastern Bank in Boston. Safety deposit box number two-seven-two."

"The Eastern Bank in Boston?" she asked, stunned. "That's where my mother-in-law banks. That's her safety deposit box. There's another ring there?"

I nodded.

Dana stared at the ring on her finger, the truth sinking deeper. "This isn't the original. These are both copies."

Annette got to her feet and helped me to mine before swiping at her wet knees, trying to remove as much mud as possible. "I'm sorry," she said to Dana.

"That woman made me believe if I lost this ring, I'd be shunned from the family for all eternity. I'd be cast out because a piece of jewelry was more valuable to her than I was."

Annette, ever the diplomat, asked brazenly, "Do you think your husband knows it's not the original?"

Her mind hadn't worked that far into the scenario, yet. The question surprised her. The implications therein. For one thing, if he had known and allowed his mother to put that kind of pressure on his wife, he was an ass. For another, whether he knew or not, he allowed his mother to put that kind of pressure on his wife, making her membership in the family contingent upon the care and feeding of a hunk of metal, which also made him an ass. Also, his name was Whittington. His first name. So, ass.

A beautiful fury erupted out of Dana. She took her phone and started punching the screen. "Let's find out."

We went back inside and Dana stepped away to speak to her husband, who was apparently boarding a flight, while Annette and I played with her wieners. It only made me want a wiener of my very own.

Dana came back a few minutes later, her fury burning just as bright. "He swears he didn't know. It doesn't matter. We are going to have a long talk when he gets home."

"Good for you," Annette said to her. "Don't take his shit."

She laughed. "I don't know how to thank you."

"Cash is always good."

"Annette!" Now it was my turn to embrace the pink glow of humiliation.

"What? You said you wanted another sandwich."

"Of course," Dana said. She started for her purse.

I stopped her. I felt wrong, suddenly, for an entirely different reason. The world tilted beneath my feet. "We'll get back to you, Dana. We need to go." I cast a desperate glare to Annette, imploring her to hurry.

She nodded, took my arm, and we headed out the back door.

"Thank you, again," Dana said as we left.

I waved and hurried for the gate. Unfortunately, we only made it halfway before my feet quit working. I fell to my knees. Annette followed.

She pushed my hair back. "Oh, no. Not again. Breathe. Breathe." Then she demonstrated, performing breathing techniques I was fairly certain were earmarked for women in labor.

And yet, they worked. Short, short, long. Short, short, long. The world slowly came back into focus. The darkened edges of my vision dissipated. And elation lifted me back onto my feet. Well, Annette lifted me back onto my feet, but elation helped.

"We did it!" I shouted to Ruthie when we got back to the house. The world spun again, just for a sec. "And," I said, tearing off my jacket in the kitchen while Annette made the brown elixir of life, "it wasn't even the original ring. I know right? Her mother-in-law has that—" I looked at my laptop screen. The video frame was there, but Ruthie wasn't. "Gigi?"

I leaned into the screen. Picked up my laptop. Shook it. "Gigi, where are you?"

Just when I was seconds away from sending for the Coast Guard, Ruthie stumbled onto the screen, her hair mussed, her clothes in disarray. "I'm here," she said, straightening her blouse. "I'm back."

Suspicion furrowed my brows. "Where were you?"

"I had to visit the little girl's room."

Annette looked perplexed. "Why would they have a little girl's room in the afterlife?"

Ruthie lifted her hair off the back of her neck with one hand and fanned her face with the other. "There aren't actual stalls."

The slight blush to her cheeks, the soft glow of her skin. It all reminded me of— "Oh, my God," I said, appalled. "Were you and Chief Metcalf just—"

"What?" she asked.

"Were you—" I could barely say the words "—did you just have cybersex with the chief?"

She dropped her hair and brushed lint off her shoulder. "I'm certain I don't know what that means."

"Online sex."

"Oh. Then, yes."

I gasped.

Annette gasped, too, but for an entirely different reason. The look of delight on her face was disturbing. "Way to go, Mrs. G!"

"I can't believe there's a word for that."

"Grandma, how is that even possible."

She fanned her face again. "That man was born with a gift, Defiance. A calling, if you will. He's carried the burden well."

I gaped a solid minute while Annette laughed beside me. "I can't hear this."

She stopped to look at me, her face bathed in soft hues. "I'm old, Defiance. I'm not dead."

"You are dead, actually. You are the definition of dead."

Annette backhanded my arm. "Hey, at least somebody's getting some. Speaking of which, you're glowing."

I pursed my lips. "I know she's glowing. That's how I knew."

"No," she said, leaning in to study me closer. "You are. What's up with that?"

I pushed away and walked to the coffee pot. "I forgot my shine-control powder, okay?"

"It's not shine. I mean, you're glowing." She followed me to the pot and leaned in again, apparently to count my pores. "It's so soft it's hardly noticeable and yet it's there." She grabbed my chin and turned my face this way and that.

"Please stop."

"She's right," Ruthie said. "I remember that from when you were a child. After a spell, you would often glow. It was subtle and radiant and quite beautiful."

"For real? Oh, well, that's cool." I brushed it off as an everyday occurrence, then added, "I have to pee." I abandoned my coffee and hurried toward the stairs.

"Please," Annette said, "you're going to see for yourself."

"Am not!" I yelled over my shoulder. But seriously, I had to see this.

I rushed up the stairs, each trip getting a little easier, and emerged on the landing only a little out of breath. When I went into the bathroom, however, I found a man under the sink again. What the hell was up with that sink?

No worries.

"Hey, I'm just going to look in the mirror."

"Oh, hold on," Roane said.

Unfortunately, I had already straddled him. "It's okay. I just have to see my glow before it disappears."

He must not have heard me, because he scooted out from under the sink and raised up just as my foot touched the ground on the other side of him. What happened next was hard to put into coherent thought.

Basically, I felt something at my crotch and my knee-jerk reaction to an intruder trying to invade the promised land without my permission was to, well, jerk my knee toward the offender.

A knee that he caught easily, his large hand wrapping around my leg and doing some kind of hand-to-hand combat maneuver. Before I knew what was happening, I'd been lifted off the ground and flipped over, landing on my back, stunned and gasping for air out of surprise. Not pain.

Then I realized he was on top of me. He'd pinned my hands above my head as his arms and legs took the brunt of his weight.

I took a moment to assess my condition. Nothing hurt, really, besides my pride.

"That was unexpected," I said between pants.

"Hmm," he agreed. His olive eyes traveled over me slowly. Methodically. The warmth they generated could've heated the Chrysler Building. "Interesting."

"What?" I asked, blowing a lock of hair out of my eyes.

"You really are glowing."

"Really?" I struggled to get out from under him.

He rose onto his booted feet and lifted me off the ground so easily, I wondered if he didn't have some kind of ability himself. Was super strength a thing in the witch world?

Then he steadied me from behind before stepping back as I leaned into the mirror. "Hmm."

"See?" He folded his arms over his chest as a lopsided grin emerged.

"I guess."

"It's not what you were expecting?"

"No. I mean, it's okay. I just thought maybe I would be bright enough to light up a room. You know, in case the power goes out."

He took a long moment to answer, and when he did, he was studying me in the mirror with great interest, his olive-green eyes searching. "You don't need magics to light up a room, Ms. Dayne."

My mouth went dry. I licked my lips and his body seemed to react. He stiffened. Stepped closer. Slid a hand around to my stomach.

I covered his with my own in a clear invitation to stay awhile, and he laced our fingers together.

Asking about his tragic past sat on the very tip of my tongue. About the fact that he didn't talk until he was seven. What would cause that? I burned to know more about this man. I also burned to turn around and plant my mouth on his. Because that's what he needed. Me taking advantage of him. How many others had done the same to him growing up?

"I found the ring," I said instead, the inane part of my brain stepping up to the mic. Then again, he did have the sexiest jawline I'd ever seen, bewhiskered as it was. It was hardly my brain's fault.

"I thought you might." He was so close now, his warm breath fanned across my cheek.

"There were three actually," I said, my voice airy.

"Ah." He seemed only half interested as he molded the length of his body to my backside.

I could hear the blood rushing in my ears. Smell the earthy scent of him. Feel the hardness at the small of my back that let me know, in no uncertain terms, he was interested.

"Did you see it?" Annette asked, barging into the bathroom.

Roane stepped back like he'd been doing something wrong.

I cleared my throat and turned on the water, hoping I wasn't about to flood the whole house. No idea what he'd been working on down there.

"Oh," she said, screeching to a halt. "I am so sorry." She showed her palms and began to back out of the room, but Roane had sobered.

"I need to run to the hardware store anyway," he said. "I'll be back in ten."

He rushed past her.

She slammed her lids shut. "I did not just do that."

"You did, actually, but it's okay. I mean, I'm not sure I should start something I can't finish."

"You can't finish? Why can't you finish it?"

"I have to decide, Nette. Today. And as much as I want to, I just can't keep Percy."

"I've been thinking about that." She lowered the lid to the toilet and sat down. "What if I sold my car?"

The befuddled look I graced her with spurred her to talk faster.

"Just hear me out. My car is paid off, right? We could sell it just to get us started. It could help us pay the utilities and taxes and all that other crap, just until we get our business going."

I snorted. "Our business? And what business would that be?"

"You! You're the business. I'm what is commonly known as the *business manager*." She added air quotes. "Or administrative assistant. I'm good with either. The icing on the cake? I have excellent phone etiquette."

She really didn't. "I don't know, Nette. I don't think I should accept money for this."

"You can't tell me Ruthie didn't earn money with her gift. A girl's gotta make a living, Deph."

I turned off the water and leaned against the sink. "I'm just such a hot mess."

"I'll see your hot mess and raise you a walking disaster."

"And Ruthie may have made money with her gift, but she was far more knowledgeable about these things than I am. She grew up in this world. I don't know the first thing about how to be a witch. About what's expected of me. What I can and cannot do."

"All of that will happen in time. You have the perfect mentor. She can teach you all the tricks. Also, you're a chef."

I lifted a brow, wondering where this was going. "I'm a restauranteur. Not a chef."

"Same dif."

Not even close. "And what does that have to do with our business?"

She rubbed her hands together a little too enthusiastically. It reminded me of a handlebarred villain in a black and white cartoon. "Now, this is just an idea, okay? One of about one hundred twelve, but I've only just started. What if we pick one day a month, say a Friday night, and have a dinner and a séance?"

"I'm sorry?"

"You cook and then do your magic. Percy pitches in with some scary haunted-house crap. Roane serves because his presence alone will fill the house. And yours truly takes the money."

"You take the money?"

"I haven't worked out all the details, but yes."

"And I just cook and do my magic?"

"That's it. Easy as pie. They'll be lining up."

"There's only one thing wrong with your plan."

She held up an index finger. "I know where you're going with this."

"Do you?"

"My car isn't worth the cost of a *For Sale* sign."

"Exactly."

"That's why we need to start charging people now. I'll get the bill typed up immediately. How does Dana spell her last name?"

"Annette," I said, appalled all over again. I was going to use up all of my appalls in one day if I wasn't careful. "We can't charge her."

"Of course we can. We single-handedly may have saved her marriage, or convinced her to leave her husband, and we found two extra rings to boot. How can we *not* charge her?"

A knock on the door saved me from having to explain all the things wrong with that question.

"What about your job?" I asked before I left.

"Managing Dr. Handsy's office staff?" Not his real name. "I think I'll survive."

She had a point. I hurried down the stairs and opened the door to the banker dude. What was his name again?

"Oh, hi." I snapped my fingers then pointed at him. "Mr. Bourne. Right. The bank robbery. I haven't forgotten you, but I have two other clients to see today. How about I drop by the bank, say, tomorrow morning?"

He held up a finger to stop me when I eased the door closed.

"I'll be there. Promise!" I shouted through the door.

I plastered my back against the thick wood and looked around at the haunting grandeur before me. "I think I love you, Percy."

The floor purred. Or Ink did. It was hard to tell since he was busy twisting his body around my ankles. I'd like to twist my body around something, too, but I couldn't do that to either of us. If I had to leave, which was the most likely scenario, I didn't want Roane thinking I was just using him for a quickie. Though I would make sure there was nothing quick about our encounter.

If I did leave, though, I'd have to drop by the bank to help Mr. Bourne before I headed out of town. How hard could it be to find bank robbers? I could only hope they were the nonviolent type.

My stomach growled, reminding me of the time. Who needed a watch when I had old faithful?

TWELVE

Don't break someone's heart.
They only have one.
Break their bones.
They have, like, 206.
-Advice from Dear Abigail

Annette and I sat with Ruthie in the kitchen and ended up in a heated debate that wasn't so much philosophical as it was conspiratorial. Or, more to the point, how to keep my gift—her words—a secret.

"I don't understand. You helped people all the time," I said, stuffing my face with a seafood salad. It took my last dime, so I was seriously hoping to sell another journal soon. "They saw you do it, right?"

"Yes," Ruthie said, "but I did it the normal way."

"I'm not sure there is such a thing," Annette said to her, then she focused on me. "What are you doing?"

I checked my Etsy account. No sales so far. I'd have to

ship the three I sold earlier the second I got home. In the meantime, I was emailing them to let them know I was out of town and would ship their orders ay-sap.

"Writing a customer. How do you spell consecrated?"

"C-o-n-s-c-u-h-k-r-a-t-e-d."

Ruthie's head was down, busy drawing something again, when she spoke absently under her breath, "Not even close."

"That doesn't look right," I told her.

She stopped eating to give me her full attention. "Look, you asked me how I spell it. Not how the dictionary spells it. Don't blame me if it doesn't look right. Why are you talking to a customer about consecration?"

"Oh, they love that stuff. My journals are made from aged materials. I like to embellish. You know, throw in little things like, "This journal is special. The leather was dyed from consecrated dirt thought to come from a vampire's coffin after a preacher from the 1800s blessed it to keep him out. But on that night, their tricks did not work. Alistair Corrigan, a 237-year-old vampire, slipped through their fingers yet again."

Annette snorted. "That's great. If you really have one like that, I call dibs."

"No, Annette. I do not have a journal made from leather dyed with consecrated vampire dirt."

"Bummer."

"Girls," Ruthie said. "Can we get back to the issue?"

"Right. Sorry." I took another bite. "So, I have to figure out how to find things without revealing how I did it?"

"Yes."

"Why is that again?" Annette asked.

"Because, we have to keep the fact that Dephne is a charmling as secret as possible."

"You're the one who told everyone in town about me. Loose lips, Gigi."

"I told them you are a powerful witch. Nothing more."

"Okay. I get part. I don't get how I'm supposed to do that when drawing the symbols is like the light show at a Pink Floyd concert."

"What are you talking about?" Annette asked.

I questioned her with my face. "The light?"

She questioned me back with her face, and I couldn't help but note that her questioning expression was way better than mine. Way more dubious.

"The light that bleeds through the lines when I draw the spells? You know, the blinding one?"

She furrowed her brows in thought. "There's a light?"

I stopped eating to focus on her. "You mean to tell me you can't see it?" I looked at Ruthie then back to Annette.

"Apparently not. I had no idea. I thought you were just waving your hand and, I don't know, like a voice came into your head and told you where the rings were."

"You've never seen the light?" I was almost offended.

"Nope."

"What about in the video of me as a child? Could you see the light from the spell?"

"There was no light. I just saw you draw in the air like you do now."

"Then why did you go into such a stupor when my powers sparked to life?"

"Because of everything else.

"Everything else?"

"Yeah. Papers flying. My hair standing straight up as tough a giant wave of static electricity shot through the house. The lights flickering. Then you screamed and doubled over and I thought something had possessed you like in *The Exorcitst.*"

"Oh. That makes sense then. But you could see me glowing."

"True." She shifted her mouth to the side. "That is weird."

"Can you see the light, Ruthie?"

She stopped drawing and held up the paper. "What does this mean?"

After a quick glance, I swallowed my latest mouthful, and said, "It's a reveal spell, just a very specific one. It reveals when a loved one or a friend has betrayed you. I get the feeling it's kind of dangerous."

"Like, dark? Is it dark magic?"

"Maybe. Why? Where did you see it?"

"I saw it in a note many years ago and I've always wondered. It's not important."

"Okay, so I have to do all of this in secret, but if no one can see the light—"

"The mundane can't."

"Hey," Annette said, pretending to be offended.

"Powerful witches and anyone of royal blood can. I can. Oh, and of course other charmlings, but the chances of you running into one of them any time in the near future are, well, let's just say you have a better chance of winning the lottery. Six times. Consecutively."

"That's it?"

"Not exactly. There are certain breeds of people who can see it. They're also few and far between. Also, if I'm not mistaken, a segment of the population with certain types of mental illness can see it."

"Good to know. Wait, did you say *breeds*?"

"People with . . . unique gifts."

"Oh." I took another bite. "Okay then. To sum up, I can do the magic just not in front of anyone who might be able to see the light and we have no way of knowing who that might be."

"Basically, though that's not what I'm talking about. If they can see the light from your spells, they will likely know what you are anyway. I mean the mundane. If they start talking, especially with today's social media platforms, word could get out."

I finished my salad and got up to rinse my plate. "What do you suggest I do then?"

"Chant."

"Chant?"

"Like I would. Make everyone believe you're just a regular witch using traditional spells and drawing your power from nature."

"What happens when I draw the spell?"

"Simply do it discreetly. Nannette," she said, looking at my BFF mid-bite,

"this is where you come in. There are any number of distractions you could employ to get their attention away from Defiance long enough for her to draw the spell."

Annette was still confused. "I can do that. But why could I see her glow?"

"That, my dear, is a good question."

A bashful laugh escaped her. She looked up at me. "She called me *my dear*."

I tried calling Mr. Touma again, the one with the missing wife. "He's still not answering. Surely they've found his wife by now. I mean, she's elderly with Alzheimer's. How hard could it be?"

"I'll check in with Houston and find out," Ruthie said.

"In the meantime, do you want to try to tackle the missing girlfriend?"

"I could try. I have his address."

"Okay, you give that a shot, as long as you did your homework first."

"Of course," I said, giving Annette a shrug. No idea what homework I was supposed to do.

She shrugged back.

"Let's take my vintage mint green Volkswagen Beetle to Wade Scott's house."

"Oh, my God. That car is going to accidentally end up in Collins Cove."

Hopefully not. It was the only thing I had left after the divorce. The only thing I'd had before I met Kyle, besides my savings that went into the restaurant. Another reason it was so special to me.

WE PULLED up to a gorgeous old building someone had turned into apartments. I checked the clock on my phone. I had four hours to decide about Percy. If I could get to Mrs. Richter's law offices before five p.m., I could back out of the deal using that law I was certain existed.

Just thinking about the decision made my stomach hurt. I loved him. Percy. And quite possibly Roane, but we were nowhere near that kind of revelation. I was too old to believe in insta-love. It wasn't that. It was him. His open-ness. His intensity. The way his arms felt around me. Like they belonged there. Like they'd been made for me and me alone.

We rang Wade Scott's buzzer. He unlocked the access

door without identifying us. We took the stairs to the third floor, so by the time we got up top, we were both panting.

Wade opened the door before we'd recovered, forcing us to control our breathing so we wouldn't look so shamefully out of shape.

"You came," he said, his expression full of hope.

And I thought Dana had been a mess. He had bed head to the extreme, but I got the feeling it was simply due to a lack of showering. His clothes were dirty and draped loosely over his thin frame.

"I can try to help, Wade. I just want you to understand, I can't make any promises."

"It's okay. I understand. Please, excuse the mess." He motioned us inside. "I've been a wreck."

We tiptoed around takeout boxes and dirty socks to a sofa loaded down with blankets and fresh laundry. At least something was clean. Poor guy.

"Please," he said, frantically cleaning the sofa off. "Can I get you anything?"

"No, thank you." I took the sofa and Annette sat on a wooden rocking chair.

He nodded, nervous, and rubbed his hands down his sweatpants. "Okay, what do I need to do?"

"Sit here." I patted the seat next to me.

He did and I took his hand in mine, turned it palm up, and waited for the spell to form in my mind. Even though I knew it, I knew the symbol, it wouldn't take shape. I couldn't make the spell work.

"I'm sorry." A nervous laugh bubbled up. "Performance anxiety."

He laughed softly. "It's okay. Take your time. I'm just so worried about her, I'm willing to try anything. If I need to do jumping jacks or sell my soul, I'm game."

"No need for that." At least I hoped not. "Is that Sara?"

One wall was covered with a woman's pictures. All candid shots. Long dark hair. Golden bronze skin. She looked South American and had the curves to prove it.

"Yeah."

"She's beautiful."

"She is." His expression turned forlorn.

"Okay, let's try this again."

He nodded and gave me his palm. "Are you reading it?"

"No. I have no idea how to read palms. I'm just trying to get a lock on where Sara is." I concentrated for a solid five minutes to no avail. Damn it. I thought I was getting the hang of this charmling stuff. I looked at Annette. "Maybe I need to be at her house instead? I don't know."

"Maybe." Her expression told a different story. I realized she was uncomfortable to the extreme.

"Wait," Wade said. "Maybe you need something of hers to help you get a read."

"Again, I've never done this. Not with a person, anyway. So, maybe."

He jumped up and disappeared into a back room.

I looked at Annette, and whispered, "What?"

"What? I didn't say anything."

"You didn't have to. What's wrong?"

"I don't know. I just get a weird feeling from this guy. You're the one with the gift, though. If you're okay, I'm okay."

I nodded, not sure I was okay with any of this.

He came back in with a necklace in his hand. "How about this?"

"It's worth a shot."

I took it into both my hands, closed my eyes, and concentrated. The spell fought me. It retreated into dark corners. I had to use all of my will to get it to come into the light. When I finally had a hold of it, I stood, turned my back on Wade, and drew it with two fingers in the air.

Light washed over me as the location spell took hold. I forgot to chant, like Gigi said, but it was all I could do just to keep a hold on the spell.

When I finished the symbol, I pushed it with my palm into the universe. Then I saw the town like a map in my mind. It found her almost instantly. I zoomed in. She was in a dive on the edge of town. I zoomed in again. No. Not in it. In a wooded area behind it.

And then I saw the tops of trees. Looking up from the forest floor, I studied the intricate patterns they made. Birds flew overhead and my heart slowed until I could no longer hear it.

My throat closed and I snapped back to the here and now. Was she dead? Did someone kill her and leave her there? If so, Wade didn't need to see that.

The spell, still fighting tooth and nail, burned my palms and I whirled around to him.

He was shielding his eyes. "That was bright."

Annette and I exchanged a furtive glance. I recovered first. "I may have something, but you stay here. We'll check it out."

"What?" He rose to his feet, anger arcing out of him. "No." He grabbed his coat. "I'm going with you."

"Wade, I don't even know if this worked. Let us check it out. Make sure it's even her, first. I'll call you the minute I know something."

He fought to stay civil. The muscles in his face were pulled taut. His jaw clenched shut. After a moment, he drew in a lungful of air and forced himself to calm. "Okay. Fine. You'll call the minute you find her?"

"Promise."

He ran a hand through his blond hair and left us alone, presumably to gather himself. Or dismiss us. Either way.

After almost falling down the stairs, the spell made me so weak, Annette drove the bug to the Palace Motel and parked on the side.

"I'll do this," I told her. "I don't know what I'm going to find. It could be bad."

"What? No. I'm going. We're in this together. Besides, you're still woozy."

I almost called Gigi then thought better of it. I could explain it all later. "Okay, but if you're scarred for life from this . . ."

"Deal. No blaming the witch."

"Right," I said with a chuckle.

We traipsed around the back of the motel and hiked into the forest. What had been so clear during the spell looked convoluted here. Out of place. However, in all honesty, my sense of direction sucked. I raised my palm and reached out to find Sara's essence, like a superhero in a movie only way less cool.

"This way."

Annette, knowing how challenged I was with the whole north-south-east-west thing, asked, "Are you certain?"

We hurried along a trail, ducking branches and swiping at leaves until we saw it. A body sprawled on the forest floor. A hand shot to my mouth, and we inched closer.

I stepped on a twig, snapped it in two, and the body reared up. The woman turned toward us, surprise evident in her every move.

Once she got a good look at us, she jumped to her feet and dusted herself off. "Sorry. This isn't what it looks like."

"What does it look like?" I asked.

"Well . . ." She struggled to answer my question and then laughed. "I guess I don't know. It's probably not every day you find a girl laying on the forest floor."

"That's true." My relief was so great, she could've been lying there in the nude and I wouldn't have cared. Not that I would've cared anyway. To each her own.

"The treetops." She pointed up.

"The treetops?" Annette asked.

"The patterns they make. I love looking at them, so I come out here. It's very soothing."

"I bet it is." I stepped forward. "I'm Defiance Dayne."

"What an unusual name."

"Yeah. I like to think I earned every syllable."

She laughed and sank onto a boulder. "I'm Sara."

"It's beautiful out here." I did a 360, taking in the scenery. It was all so different from the A-Z.

"It is," she said. "Are you staying at the motel?"

Annette and I looked at each other. The more I studied the situation, the more I found wrong with it. Sara was clearly not being held against her will, unless her captors were just really trusting. Or she was totally cool with it.

I'd brought out my phone to text Wade. Instead, I noticed several texts from a number I didn't recognize.

"Is everything okay?"

I bounced back to her. "Yes. Sorry. No, we aren't staying at the hotel. Sara, we've actually been hired by, well, we think by your boyfriend. He said you've been missing."

Her face visibly paled and she shot to her feet. "Wade?" she asked, her gaze darting about.

"Don't worry." I raised my palms. "He doesn't know where you are."

"Wade hired you?"

"Yes. I'm guessing that's a bad thing. Again, he doesn't know—"

"Trust me. If you're here, he knows."

"Yes, he does," came a male voice. I pivoted around to see Wade behind us on the trail. He'd followed us.

This was not happening.

He was holding a knife at his side. A hunting knife like Rambo's.

Sara drew a gun out of her jacket. A small semi-automatic she'd clearly bought for protection against this man. She pointed it at him, her hands shaking so much I was afraid she would hit me or Annette.

He tsked her. "Sweetheart, I know how I die. I saw it when I was a kid, remember?" He gestured toward the gun. "And that ain't it."

"I have no intention of killing you. Hurting you, however . . ."

Annette eased toward me and looped her arm in mine.

"What's going on?" I asked.

"He's not my boyfriend," Sara said, her voice full of hate and fear. "We used to work together, but he started stalking me."

I welded my teeth together. This was what Ruthie meant by *homework*. How could I be so stupid? "This is why you're here."

"Yes. I just wanted some peace. I just wanted to feel safe for five minutes. Drop the knife, Wade."

"And did she tell you about when we first met?" he asked, growing vehement himself. "How she smiled and flirted with me?"

He kept inching closer to us. Annette and I eased to the side. He cast us a warning glare, so we stopped. But I still had my phone in my hands. I tried to dial 911 with only a glance at my phone, and I had no idea if it worked.

"I smiled, Wade," Sara said, "because I'm a nice person. I smile at everyone."

He took another step, his anger rising if his splotchy complexion were any indication. "You told me you liked me."

"I felt sorry for you. I thought everyone avoided you because of your poor social skills. Then I figured out your social skills were exactly where you wanted them to be. You're an asshole, plain and simple."

He rushed forward, pointing the knife at her accusingly. "And you're a bitch, just like the rest of them. You flirt when you want something and ignore when you don't."

Sara put her finger on the trigger. He stopped, but at only a few feet away, still far too close for comfort. He could do a lot of damage before the bullets even fazed him.

He tilted his head and grinned. "I told you, babe. I don't die by a gun."

Then he turned toward Annette and me, his face the picture of evil, and lunged forward, plunging the knife into my ribcage.

THIRTEEN

Can anyone tell me if
"the skulls of your enemies"
are dishwasher safe?
-Q&A Forum for the Modern Housewife

I figured out somewhere between that first knife thrust and the second that he was simply trying to disable me so he could use me as a shield to get to Sara. He jerked me forward. At the same time, Annette fell back, taking me with her, so the knife slicing into my flesh didn't hit the mark he'd intended.

We screamed as we fell. We screamed harder when he tried to get me back onto my feet. Thankfully, Annette had a death grip.

Frustrated, he did the next best thing. He went after me again with the knife. Two quick thrusts, though both were deflected by the bulkiness of my winter coat, then he went after Annette.

As though in slow motion, I watched as the silver blade plunged downward Before it hit its target, a.k.a. Annette's shoulder, Wade was ripped off us. A thunderous burst of sound, deep and guttural, ricocheted off the trees around us.

At first, I thought Sara had fired the gun. Then I realized, Wade had been ripped off us by a dog.

We scrambled to our feet and watched in horror as the dog—no, the wolf—ripped into Wade, its bone-chilling growl the stuff of nightmares. As were Wade's screams.

My hands shot to my mouth as the wolf tore into his flesh, the frenzy like nothing I'd ever seen. Like a shark's. Fierce. Frantic. Feverish.

It was massive, its red coat thick and shimmering.

Then I realized Wade still had the knife. He buried it into the wolf's side. All he got for his efforts was a sharp yelp and a mouth full of teeth clamping down on his arm. He screamed again as the wolf, still in an absolute frenzy, lunged for his throat.

He raised his arm just in time. The wolf's teeth cut deep grooves into his face instead.

I couldn't watch any longer. I ran to Sara, took the gun, and fired it into the air.

To my surprise, the wolf jolted and turned toward me, its enormous teeth bloodied and bared as it took me in. I tried to point the gun at it, just in case, but I was shaking so hard I could barely hold it steady.

Then I registered sirens. With a quick glance over my shoulder, I saw a line of police vehicles charging toward us using the riverfront access road.

The wolf examined his whimpering victim, sniffed him, then huffed out a breath, as though his scent had been offensive.

Without another thought for its victim, it turned and

trotted deeper into the forest, but not before I got a good look at the gash in his side and the blood dripping off him. I made a mental note to call the game warden. Then again, maybe not. They'd surely destroy him for attacking a human.

Sara sank onto the forest floor and vomited as a small army descended upon the scene.

Annette's senses began to clear faster than mine did, and she ran to Wade who lay mewling in a fetal position.

"Do you die by a wolf?" she asked, kicking his leg. "Is that how you die, creep?"

A nice police officer with pecs to die for pulled her off him while the EMTs checked his wounds.

"Is that how you die?" she yelled as the officer lifted her off the ground and dragged her kicking and screaming toward a patrol car, her hair a box of springs, her glasses askew.

God I loved her.

When Chief Metcalf put his hands on my shoulders and looked into my eyes, presumedly to check for shock— either that or he picked a fine time to notice the blue in my eyes—I pointed past him, and said simply, "Knife."

"Hold!" he shouted. The EMTs scrambled back when they realized there was a knife underneath Wade's leg. Surprisingly, Wade was smart enough not to go for it.

Another officer swooped in and put the knife in an evidence bag, while a third checked on Sara.

"Defiance?" the chief said, as though talking to a child. Or a suicide bomber. "Sweetheart, you're hurt. Let's get you to the ambulance, okay?"

"Wolf," was all I could manage.

"Okay, sure. We'll get you a wolf, but first let's get you checked out." Though he was teasing, I wondered if they'd seen the magnificent, nightmarish thing. The thing from my dreams. The hauntingly beautiful beast that just saved my life.

Even as they laid me on a gurney, I wondered.

After a few minutes of oxygen, I was good as new. If not for the convulsive like shaking, the bile burning the back of my throat, and the two gashes in my side—thank God for my parka—I was good to go.

I lay in the back of an ambulance while an older rascally EMT named Chad checked my vitals for the twelve-thousandth time.

Annette sat beside him, having given up her life of vengeance, and the chief sat beside her. It was quite cozy.

"Care to explain?" the chief asked me.

"I didn't check out his story." I looked from Annette to him through tear-filled lashes. "Why didn't I check out his story? I could've gotten her killed."

"Correction. *We* could've gotten her killed," Annette said. "I'm already slipping on the job and we haven't even officially opened."

The chief took my hand. "It's okay, daffodil. Even your grandmother made mistakes." I suddenly saw the sadness in his eyes.

"You really love her." And why wouldn't he? She was beautiful and fascinating and smart.

"I do."

"Do you mind me asking why you never married?"

His laugh was breathy and a little heartbreaking. "I asked. Month after month. Year after year. She was too classy to lead me on. She simply told me no. Every time."

"Why? She loves you, too. I can tell."

"She was meant for greater things. I knew that. I just wanted to be a part of her life."

"You were. You still are, oddly enough."

His nod was unconvincing.

"Hey, how did you know to come? Did my call get through?" I took out my phone. Instead of dialing 911, I'd dialed 744645802370000002.

So close.

"No. Your grandmother sent me."

"She sent you?"

This time his nod was more of a sheepish believe-it-or-not.

"And how did she do that exactly?"

"She, um—" he lifted a hesitant shoulder "—she texted me."

"She texted you?" Surprised, I opened the texts I'd gotten earlier. "I think she texted me, too. How on planet Mars did she manage that?" She'd sent me about 30 texts, all of them warning me not to go to Wade's apartment. "She can't possibly get cell reception in the veil."

"I checked Wade out. Seems he was a suspect in a missing persons case last year in Ipswich. A young female who looks startlingly similar to Sara. The case was never solved." He watched as the ambulance carrying Wade's quivering body drove away. "Maybe now it will be."

"How is Sara?"

"She's good," Annette said. "She's grateful."

"I'm glad."

"Me too. I'll type up a bill."

"Annette," I began, but she giggled.

I giggled back and soon what started out as a simple release of near-death tension turned into the infamous gigglefest of unprecedented nature, an uncontrollable monstrosity that defined vulgar and inappropriate at the same time.

The chief, laughing himself, started to leave. I stopped him and said through the tears, "I've been asked to find Jameel Touma's wife. Is she really missing?"

"I'm afraid so. She's been gone since early this morning. It's not looking good."

"I was afraid you'd say that."

ANNETTE POUNDED on the bathroom door. "Look," she said, her voice raised, "I get why you didn't go to the hospital. You need stitches but you'll live. What I don't get is why you've been in the bathroom for the past hour."

Apparently, PTSD could strike instantly after a traumatic event. We hurried home to change and go back out to help Mr. Touma when I caught a glimpse of the gashes in my side. That was when it hit me. I could've gotten Sara killed. And Annette. And a gorgeous wolf who could be dying at that very moment. I sat on the edge of the tub, my limbs to shaky to hold my weight, waiting to make sure I wasn't going to heave.

Another knock sounded at the door.

"I'm almost finished," I said, eyeing the toilet just in case. "And after this, I'm going back out to find the wolf." I made a mental list of the equipment I would need.

A male voice drifted through the door. "Dephne, sweetheart."

I bolted off the tub, opened the door, and flew into the open arms of my dads.

"What are you guys doing here?" I asked, the joy I felt like tiny hearts bursting all around me.

Papi, the younger of the two, whirled me around as Dad looked on with a smile on his handsome face.

"Cariña," Dad said, his serious demeanor ever-present despite the grin, "we wouldn't miss this for anything."

They led me down the stairs. "This house," Papi said. "I'm in love."

"His name is Percival. What are you guys doing here? Why didn't you tell me you were coming?"

They shared a quick glance and Papi shook his head.

"What?" I asked.

"Nope. That's for your dad to explain. I had nothing to do with it."

We sat in the living room, Papi beside me on the sofa and Dad in the wingback as Annette brought out a tray of coffee, really getting into this assistant thing.

She grabbed her cup and sat in the second wingback.

"Did you know they were coming?" I asked her.

"No idea." Having had a crush on him since high school, she beamed at my older dad. "But I'm glad."

"Me too. So," I said, eyeing Dad suspiciously, "what is there to explain?"

He reached into his pocket and brought out a letter. "This is for you." He handed it to me then leaned in to make him a cup. Papi did the same, purposely avoiding eye contact.

I opened it and began to read. I stopped immediately and frowned at them. "I don't understand."

"Just read, cariña."

MY DEAREST DEFIANCE,

If you are reading this, we have not yet met and I have crossed into the veil. I will try to find a way to communicate with you once I am there. If I fail, I have left explicit instructions with your fathers that must be followed to the letter.

Trust them in the coming days. Lean on them for guidance. You are in grave danger, my darling girl, and I can no longer protect you.

And know this. You are loved. Beyond measure. Forever and always.

Every piece of my heart,
Ruthie Goode
Your Grandmother

I SAT A LONG MOMENT, steeping in a sea of confusion. Then I looked up at the two men I trusted most in the world. "Exactly how did you know Ruthie?"

Dad bit down, his bronze skin paler than usual. "She helped save Papi's life. We owed her everything."

My body couldn't decide which emotion to settle on. Astonishment and dismay warred with a sprinkling of betrayal. Though it was only a hint, it stung, the pain sharp and precise, perfectly slicing through the center of my heart. They'd never told me. They knew who my only living relative was and never told me.

I folded the letter and slid it back into the envelope, buying time. All I could think to ask was, "Why didn't you tell me about her?"

Papi reached over took my hand. "She asked us not to. After everything she told us, we agreed."

His image blurred as wetness formed between my lashes. I glanced at Annette who sat with her cup hovering at her mouth.

Then I swallowed back the lump in my throat, and asked, "What did she tell you?"

"She told us—" he paused and took a sip "—she told us what you are."

My breath hitched. "You mean, you've known all this time?"

"We have," Dad said. Always the pragmatic. The practical one. The no-nonsense businessman who had all the answers all the time. The one, if I wasn't mistaken, who'd never believed in the spiritual world. In magic or miracles or premonition.

"And . . . and you're okay with it?"

"Of course." Papi leaned in for a quick squeeze.

I looked at Dad. "You don't believe in any of this. What do you call it? Mumbo jumbo?"

He had the decency to look guilty. "It was all part of the plan."

"To . . . to lie to me?"

He looked away and explained. "Papi had gone hiking in the Sonoran alone. He fell down an embankment and was injured.

I looked over at him. At the beautiful man I loved more than air.

Dad rested a fist over his mouth. It was clearly an emotional subject. "Search teams scoured the area for three days to no avail. I'd heard about Ruthie from a friend. I took a private jet that very night and knocked on her door at three in the morning." He looked up at me. "Do you know what she said to me?"

I'd scooted to the edge of my seat. "What?"

"She looked me up and down, and said, 'You're late.'"

A hint of laughter bubbled out of me. "I can see her saying that. So, she saved Papi's life?"

"She . . . didn't, actually." The look he placed on me, the element of absolute gratitude, told me what he was going to say before the words left his mouth. His grave expression turned even more solemn, and he said, "You did."

I didn't know I had a hand over my mouth until I went to talk. I lowered it and said, "I saved him?"

Papi, with his gilded hair and crystalline blue eyes, took my hand into his. "You saved my life. You don't know how long I've waited to thank you."

He pulled me into a deep hug and I melted against him until another thought hit me.

I leaned back. "Is that why you agreed to take me in? Because you owed me?"

"Defiance, you can't honestly believe that. It's true we were beyond honored that she chose us to care for her most valuable possession, but we did it because we grew to love you."

"We visited often after that," Dad said. "Trust me when I say Ruthie knew what she was doing. We came almost every month for a year."

"A year? How old was I when I saved you, Papi?"

"You were two."

Even younger than I had been in the video. "So, Ruthie didn't blackmail you into taking me, then?" I laughed softly, even though the potential answer made me nervous.

Dad stood. This stoic, unflappable man, this gentle giant, stood and pulled me roughly into his arms, crushing me against his chest. My favorite place to be crushed.

"We were afraid, *mi'ja*. Every day we worried Ruthie would want you back. She would change her mind. So we cherished every moment with you."

A sound escaped me that was half laugh and half sob. "Even the moment I accidentally shaved your head while you were sleeping?"

"Not that moment, but every other moment, for sure."

I squeezed so tight, I was sure I'd break his ribs, then I paused again and pushed away from him. "Wait a minute."

Anger suddenly flared inside me. "That time I wanted to join Wicca, you wouldn't let me. You said it was against God."

Again with the glances. Papi finally spoke up. "We were worried you would trigger your powers."

"You were always so drawn to all things magical," Dad said. "You have no idea how often we ran interference."

Wow. My dads knew. All this time, they knew and worked hand-in-hand with Ruthie to keep me oblivious. Not to mention free from danger.

"So, you're staying?" Papi asked, scanning the room. "You're keeping Percival?"

I felt my shoulders deflate. "I don't think so. I don't know how I can, Papi. I can't afford him."

The look of surprise on his face told me that was not the answer he was expecting.

"What else is going on?" Dad asked, ever perceptive.

I chewed on the inside of my cheek. I was in my forties and I still felt like a little girl when they were around. They were my superheroes. I hated to disappoint them, but . . . "I don't know if I can be this person. I almost got three people and a wolf killed today."

"A wolf?" Papi asked.

"And the wolf may die anyway."

"Cariña," Dad said, an edge to his deep voice, "you have a calling. It's not something to be taken lightly."

"I know. I'll try to rise to the occasion. I'll just have to do it in my own time in a place with a little less upkeep."

They nodded hesitantly. They did that a lot.

Still, their presence was a calming force. A salve. I felt like I could tackle another spell. Hopefully without passing out. There was still a woman out there who needed saving, just like Papi did.

While I wanted the whole story, Mrs. Touma didn't have much time if Ruthie's constant texting telling me to hurry was any indication. I would so take her phone away if she had one.

I stood. They followed suit, like I knew they would.

"I have to use my new gift to find a missing woman named Siham."

"We know, cariña."

Papi socked me softly on the arm, pride evident in his smile. "Atta girl."

A bashful shrug overtook me. Honestly, I was twelve again. "How long are you guys here for? Percy has, like, a thousand rooms but only ours has a bed in it. We could always buy—"

"We've already reserved a room," Papi said. "We wouldn't dream of intruding. Besides, we have to explore the town again. We haven't been here in forty years." He looked at Dad. "I wonder if that restaurant on Wharf is still here."

"Let's find out." They leaned in for a quick kiss and my heart burst with joy. Even though they were busy with the vineyard, they always made time for each other.

They got up to leave. I stopped them for one last announcement. "When you come over later, there's someone I want to introduce you to." When they exchanged curious glances, I added, "Or should I say, reintroduce you to."

"We look forward to it," Dad said.

We did another round of hugs before they took off, then I looked at the grandfather clock, the one that looked like it barely survived a fire, it was so dark. Almost 3 p.m. I didn't have much time before I had to get to Mrs. Richter's office to cancel the contract.

The way I saw it, I could cancel the contract and then think on it a few days more. It would give me some time to come up with a plan. Annette, God bless her, could've been onto something earlier. But that would have to wait.

"Ready?" I asked her.

She stood, straightened her shoulders, and tugged at the hem of her shirt. "All systems are go, Captain."

"So, yes."

She nodded. "Affirmative."

I giggled on the inside. Such a freak.

FOURTEEN

If you think women are the weaker sex,
try pulling the blankets back to your side.
-Meme

Annette called Chief Metcalf on the way over to Mr. Touma's house. They could have found his wife already, which would be wonderful. Unfortunately, that was not the case.

"You're going to try?" the chief asked over speaker-phone, his voice infused with hope.

"Yes. We're on our way. Chief, I can't promise—"

"I know. Thanks, daffodil." A warmth spread over me at his endearing term. I wondered if he'd called me that as a kid.

We pulled up to a small but well-maintained house. Two patrol cars were parked in front. One was the chief's. He came out, his expression dire.

"He's in bad shape, daff. Just wanted to warn you."

"Thank you."

"We're afraid she's in the water somewhere. Maybe got swept out to sea."

My heart sank. If I'd mastered this earlier instead of messing around. If I'd listened to Ruthie . . .

"I understand."

With a nod of encouragement, he escorted us inside. Mr. Touma was standing at a window that overlooked the water, and the chief's words became much more plausible.

"Mr. Touma?" I said, approaching him slowly.

He turned to me, his dark skin ashen, his eyes red-rimmed. He didn't remember me. He'd gone to the house expecting to see Ruthie, so it was no wonder. And I couldn't imagine how many people had come and gone from his house since Siham's disappearance.

"We spoke this morning? I'm Ruthie's granddaughter."

"Ruthie?" His face lit up until he remembered. "She's gone."

"Yes. I'll try to help if you'd like me to."

A spark of hope lit his face. "Please, yes. She's been gone for hours. What can I do?"

"I'll let you know. Is this hers?" I asked, pointing to a shawl.

He nodded.

The cop that had dragged Annette off of Wade Scott, thus saving the man's life at the rate she'd been going, was there, too. He looked on curiously until Chief Metcalf sent him out of the room.

Disappointed, he nodded and went to wait outside. But not before giving Annette a quick once-over. He did it inconspicuously. Annette didn't even notice. I damned sure did.

I had my impression of Mr. Touma. He presented as a

distraught loving husband. Still, there was always that chance he'd harmed his wife.

That was where Annette came in. I stepped to her. "What are your impressions?"

She did a doubletake as though wondering who I was talking to. "Me?" she asked, pointing to herself.

"You have a much better sense of people than I do. If I'd listened to you with Wade, I would never have put Sara's life in danger. From now on, you're in charge of initial reactions and gut instincts, which I clearly lack."

"I just don't trust anyone," she said, lifting a shoulder. "Makes things simple."

"And there you go."

"Okay, but does this promotion come with a raise? I have children to feed."

"You have a gerbil named Luke Skywalker."

"And?"

I laughed softly. "Okay. I'll give you a ten percent raise. No," I said, holding up a finger, "make it twenty."

"Sweet. Twenty percent of nothing is . . ." She did the math in the air.

"Exactly. It sounds good in theory, though."

"It does. For the record, I think Mr. Touma is a man grieving deeply over his missing wife. He would never hurt her. Look at this place."

I scanned the room. While tidy, it was a bit cluttered with knickknacks, embroidery hoops, and knitting needles.

"It's practically a shrine to his wife. His whole life revolves around her. Deph, if we don't find Mrs. Touma, he won't be far behind."

So, two deaths on my head because I couldn't get my act together sooner. Wonderful.

"Thank you."

I picked up the shawl and stepped to the middle of the room. The moment I touched it, before I even started the spell, a coldness came over me, and I tumbled into Mrs. Touma's world.

She was surviving on her baser instincts. Get out of the cold. Drink water. Find shelter from the wind. Fear reigned over her every move. Her every scattered thought.

Shivering, I watched as my breath fogged on the air. The room turned an icy blue and frost crept across the furniture, the ice crystals shimmering and crackling in the frigid air.

I raised a tremoring hand, drew the spell, and pushed it into what I was beginning to understand was the veil. The spiritual realm all around us. Before I could find her, Mrs. Touma's thoughts tugged at me. Unable to get my footing, I slipped under and fought just to stay conscious. I knew I would die if I didn't.

Don't let go.

Then I saw it. I whirled around. Metal encased me on all sides, the walls dark. Industrial. The smell of brine and steel and animal feces overpowering. And my arm hurt. Pain shot through me like nothing I'd ever felt.

Don't let go.

Mostly, the cold sliced into me. It cramped my muscles, my feet turning in on themselves, the cold so merciless.

But I couldn't let go. The monsters would get me if I let go.

"Defiance!"

I heard a voice. Male. Powerful. My lids snapped open and I was on my knees, backed into a corner in Mr. Touma's living room. I had both hands in front of me as though fending off an attack.

"Defiance," the chief said. He took hold of my shoulders and lifted me up. I stumbled but he kept a strong hold.

"Something's wrong," I said, panicked. "She's not in water, but it's nearby. She's in a warehouse." I pleaded with him. "We have to hurry."

The chief left the officer in charge of Mr. Touma and we took his cruiser.

"I can't pinpoint her location." I held my head with both hands to try to force it to calm. "It's like chaos."

Annette was in the backseat, nearing a state of panic. "This is worse than that time I ran over that kid with a golf cart."

"Since you barely bumped him, I'm going to say, yes, Annette. This is definitely worse."

"Just tell me where to go, sweetheart."

"Breathe," Annette said. "Remember to Lamaze."

My thoughts somersaulted again and I squeezed my eyes shut. "She's so cold."

"I'm going toward the port. Does anything look familiar?"

But I couldn't open my eyes without the horizon tilting. Without getting seasick.

"Defiance!" Annette said, forcing me to listen. "Deep breaths. Slow your heart. Think about the yoga instructor we hated so much and everything she taught us. Meditate. Clear your mind."

Bizarrely, Annette was getting through. I concentrated on my heartbeat. On the sound of blood in my ears. On the pulse at my neck.

"There," I said, pointing to our right.

My eyes weren't open, so the chief said, "Here? You're sure?"

I nodded. I could see her clearly now, and although I was still in her mind, I could finally control just how much.

When I lifted my head and saw the size of the warehouse, I almost lost hope. "It's huge."

"It is. We may have to split up. I'll call in more help, too." He slid to a stop by a side door that faced the waterfront.

"We'll meet you inside."

Annette and I hurried toward the entrance. There were men working in one small section. We rushed up to them.

Annette took charge. "There's a woman missing. She's lost and disoriented. We think she's in here. Can you help us look?"

The foreman nodded and a sharp whistle split the air as he called his workers over. While she explained the situation, I wandered toward the racket in my head.

This was different from the first two spells. Ruthie told me each time she used a spell it created its own special twist. She wasn't kidding.

"Hey," someone called out to me. "You can't go back there without a helmet."

I felt a helmet magically appear on my head. It wasn't the spell. Someone put one on me. I kept walking. Searching. So cold. The metal was so cold.

The chief came in and I heard him talking to the foreman. "We have more officers coming. Just send them this way."

The mammoth structure, made for working on ships, had offices and small rooms off to the sides. My arm started aching again, I just couldn't figure out why. And I was up so high.

Realization dawned and I looked up. Whirled around.

Mrs. Touma was somewhere above. Somewhere with a floor but without one.

"What does that even mean?" I asked the air.

"What are you seeing?" Annette asked.

"She's somewhere with a floor but without one. She's somewhere high because there are monsters below her feet. Teeth and claws."

"Rats!" she said. "There are rats below her."

I stopped and nodded at her. "Yes. The space is cramped yet it goes on forever.

It hit us both at the same time, and we said simultaneously, "An elevator shaft."

We turned and Annette yelled. "An elevator shaft! Where?"

The foreman jogged up, pointing to a gate about fifty feet in front of us. "She can't be in there. The gates are locked. The elevator hasn't worked in weeks."

That was it. "Chief, can you go up a couple of floors? We'll look down here."

He nodded, took one of the workers, and hurried for the stairs.

We rushed to the gates but could hardly see into the darkness beyond. Unfortunately, we could hear. Rats squeaked just beyond the metal grating.

The foreman grabbed a flashlight from his belt and shoved a hand through the gate.

"Wait," I said a microsecond before he turned it on. "It could startle her. She could fall."

Amazingly, he listened to me. Hoping beyond hope she couldn't see my light, I put my hand into the gate and drew an illumination spell.

"There." On the maintenance ladder about fifty feet up,

Siham Touma was clasping the rungs. Her fragile body shivering. Her strength waning.

Though she'd wrapped an arm around a rung, she was losing her grip on both consciousness and the ladder. The cold had twisted her muscles, drained her of her will to survive until she could hold on no longer.

And she slipped soundlessly to her death.

One minute, I watched in horror as her gown flapped in the air, the fall impossibly fast. The next minute I stood under her, palms raised as she hovered over my head. She was enveloped in a soft glow as though time itself were basking in her presence. Her gown billowed around her. Her gray hair floating as though she were in water.

I lowered her slowly to the cement ground. The rats had disbursed. Their excrement, however, had not. There was nothing I could do about that now.

The moment her feet touched the ground, I wrapped my arms around her to steady her. She didn't hesitate. She curled her arms around my waist, but her body was warm now.

"Mrs. Touma," I said, holding her with one arm while ripping my coat off with the other. I switched arms and after a struggle that would've made Houdini proud, wrapped it around her shoulders. "Your husband sent me."

"Jameel?" she asked, her voice as fragile as her mind. "He sent me an angel?"

I smiled and turned to help her out of the shaft only to come face-to-face with Annette and the foreman.

Both stood mannequin-still, their mouths agape. Unlike most mannequins.

"Are they angels, too?" she asked.

With an amused grin, I nodded. "That they are. Be careful of the curly-haired one. She's more angel-adjacent."

"Okay," she said, believing every word of it. "Sweetheart, why are we here again?"

I pulled her closer, trying not to cringe at the thought of her bare feet in the filth below us. "We're here because someone decided to go on a walkabout."

"Me, right?"

"Yes. Hey, at least you got your money's worth. This warehouse is cool."

There was a step up to get out of the shaft, but the two gawkers stood gawking and were absolutely no use whatsoever.

"Don't help or anything," I said, teasing them.

I got Mrs. Touma up to the step just as a group of workers ran up to us. They helped her first then lifted me out. "Thank you."

Then they looked at their foreman. "I think you broke Bob," one of them said.

Bob the foreman had yet to move. Had yet to blink. He only managed one word. "How?"

Annette recovered about the time I noticed some of the workers examining a wall. Or, more to the point, the gate to the elevator that had lodged into the wall. The metal wall. The one with a gate sticking out of it perpendicular to said wall.

"Wow," I said, covering my ass. "That's so weird."

Annette followed my gaze and her eyes rounded even more. She sucked in a sharp breath, then coughed before playing it off. "That is weird, Defiance. Maybe we should go before anything else weird happens. Like that microburst of wind that ripped that metal gate right off its metal hinges."

Chief Metcalf slid to a stop in front of us as one of his officers took charge of Mrs. Touma. Apparently, the cavalry had arrived and Officer Pecs had taken point.

The chief looked from me to the gate to Mrs. Touma then back to me. "Gosh," he said, rubbing his close-cropped head. "You don't see that every day."

"Right?" Annette released a nervous laugh. "Well, I guess we should go."

"Wait." Mrs. Touma raised her hand to me. The officer had brought a folding chair and sat her in it so he could wrap her head-to-toe in a blanket. Then he took off his own jacket and put it under her bare feet to wait for the ambulance. If the sirens were any indication, it was almost there.

The men were talking and pointing and looking back at me. Bob had yet to move.

I knelt beside her and she put a hand on my face. "You're still glowing."

"I know." I waved a dismissive hand. "I left my shine-control powder at home."

She laughed softly. But when she touched me, I didn't feel the confusion I'd felt before. I felt clarity. I felt the fogless, razor-sharp mind of her youth.

"Siham?" a man said from behind me.

I turned to see Mr. Touma.

"Oh, Jameel." She raised her arms and he bent to hug her. "I was so scared. I couldn't remember where I was and then I was bathed in warm light."

He reared back and studied her. "You recognize me?"

A knowing smile lit her beautiful face. "Of course, I do."

Annette and I stepped away. Quickly. Before the questions avalanched. I knew we had a connection for life, Mrs. Touma and I.

"So, way to go," Annette said. "Let's not draw attention to ourselves and send out a beacon to every evil witch within a thousand-mile radius."

"I know, I know. Let's just get out of here."

"By the way." She stopped and turned me by my shoulders to face her. "Wow."

"How much of that did you see?"

"None of it. It happened too fast. Well, maybe a little of a floating woman, but that could be chalked up the to the microburst."

We headed out the door again before I realized we had no vehicle. Where was a vintage mint green Volkswagen Beetle when I needed one?

"And just where did that come from? The microburst?" I asked her.

She shrugged.

"Genius. Pure, unmitigated genius. You're getting another raise. No," I said, holding up my palm. "Don't try to talk me out of it."

The wind cut me to the bone the minute we stepped out, and I remembered I'd given my coat to Mrs. Touma. That was the last thing I remembered, other than the pavement rushing toward my face. Damn spells.

FIFTEEN

I'm giving up drinking for a month.
Sorry, bad punctuation.
I'm giving up. Drinking for a month.
-Meme

The smell of coffee, along with my dad's deep voice, lured me out of the most blissful sleep I'd had in years. I groaned and pulled the comforter over my head.

"I'm telling you, cariña, you're going to want some of this. It's the best coffee I've ever had. Ethiopian, I think. Papi and I found it in a little shop on Wharf."

He was right. Damn it. I lowered the comforter and smiled up at my handsome dad. Or, well, dads, as they were both in my room and I was back in elementary school, when they would wake me up in the mornings together, only they didn't do it with coffee. Back then, it was chocolate milk or bust.

I scooted back and rested against the headboard, only

realizing then that I was not in my room in Arizona. Ruthie's artifacts lay strewn around me, which meant Annette had probably been sleeping next to me. A quick glance assured me she was already up.

"What time is it?" I asked, taking a cup from Papi, his blond hair still wet from a recent shower. "And why is your hair wet? Is your hotel room that close?"

"We showered here. We've been staying in a guest room."

I snorted. "That couldn't have been comfortable. There are no beds in the guest rooms."

He flashed me a nuclear smile. "There are now. We found an incredible antique shop."

"Several really," Dad said.

"Several, and we took it upon ourselves to—"

"Wait." I put the cup down and hoisted myself into a better position. "How long have I been asleep. What time is it?"

Papi looked at his watch. "It's seven p.m. Give or take."

"Oh, my God." I jumped out of bed and searched frantically for my clothes. Any clothes. A hazmat suit would do. "Where are my clothes?"

"We're doing laundry."

"Oh, no. I mean, thank you. Of course. I just need to get to Mrs. Richter's. Today's the last day I can back out of the contract."

"And why is that?" Dad asked, giving me a dubious look.

"Three days. Isn't that the law? You have three days to change your mind after you've signed a contract?"

I found a pair of sweat pants and a Three Doors Down T-shirt. No idea who they belonged to, but they'd do. And I called dibs on the TDD shirt. The room spun a little as I bounced out of my pajamas and into the sweat pants, heedless of my dads looking on. They'd certainly seen me in worse situations.

"Okay, first off," Papi said when I lost my balance and fell into the wall headfirst, "why are you trying to back out of the contract? And second off, why do you think you have three days to do it?"

I recovered but stopped mid-bounce. "Because. There's a law. Right?" My heart started to race. Had I been wrong? Wasn't there a law?

"Well, there are those types of laws. They're different for each state. Even if Massachusetts has such a law, it takes a lot to get a real estate contract reverted. In other words, you'd better have a really good reason."

After straightening and dropping the sweats, I hobbled to the bed, dragging one pant leg behind me. "No way. I was counting on that law. I would never have signed the papers had I known I couldn't get out of it."

Percy shook the floor, rattling a lamp on Ruthie's nightstand.

"Why, *mi'ja?*"

"It's not you, Percy. I just can't do right by you. You need someone who can take care of you. As much as I love you, love doesn't pay the taxes." Then I turned to my dads. "My neighbor has already offered to buy him. Parris Hamilton."

Percy shook the walls even harder. Dust filtered from the ceiling.

My dads looked around but didn't seem too alarmed. "Yes, we met her. According to Ruthie's will, Percival can't be sold for a year either way."

"I know. Then what? He would just sit here with no one to take care of him?"

They shrugged. I'd have to ask her what she'd been thinking with that little stipulation.

"And, I think you're going to want to see this." Papi took a check out of his wallet and tried to hand it to me.

I held up a hand. "No. I can't take your money."

Dad stood. "You and your pride, cariña."

"Dad, it's not pride. I just can't keep coming to you for my every need."

"Why? When we took you in, we made an oath."

"Did that oath bind you for the rest of eternity? That hardly seems fair."

Papi cleared his throat and slid a quick glare at Dad. "What your father means, sweetheart, is that this isn't our money. It's yours."

"Right." I took the check and stilled. $50,000. "What the hell? I can't accept this. Are you crazy?"

"I told you." He took my hand. "It's yours. It's the first installment to pay you back for your half of the restaurant."

"The restaurant?" I stood and paced, dragging the leg along with me.

"If you'd told us what was going on," Dad said, his Latino accent thicker now with irritation, "none of that would have ever happened."

"How did you get this?"

"It's a little thing called a good lawyer. Cariña, you let them walk all over you. We taught you better than that."

Shame burned through me. They really had taught me better. "It was my bed," I said, repeating the same motto I'd adopted since I was served divorce papers. On the day of our fifth wedding anniversary, no less.

"If you ever say something that inane to me again, I'll bend you over my knee."

"Dad, I'm forty-four."

"I didn't say it would be easy."

Laughter trickled out of me. "I don't know what to say. This means I can keep him. I can keep Percy, but then I'll be across the country from you."

"I don't know. We've been eyeing a farmhouse for sale in Ipswich."

"Really?" I asked in disbelief. "You'd move here?" When they only grinned at each other, I lunged forward and hugged them. "What about the vineyard?"

"Ricardo practically runs it anyway. Has for years."

Then another thought hit me. I stood and waved the check at them. "How did all of this happen so fast?"

"Told you. Good lawyers."

"Dad." I gave him my best dubious scowl. "Those cartel ties from your past didn't have anything to do with this, did they?"

"Cartel is a very strong word for what I was involved with in my youth. And, no. I told you. A good lawyer will do wonders."

"Then, I don't get it. They were just here, like, yesterday, threatening to take Percy from me."

That was the wrong thing to say. Dad's face turned an unhealthy shade of fuchsia. Not that there was a healthy one. "They did what?"

"Nothing. They were just being dicks. Chief Metcalf ran them out of town. But that doesn't answer my question."

Papi patted the bed beside him. "Sweetheart, sit down."

I sat beside him again, then bent and put my other leg in before it got awkward.

"Honey, you've been unconscious for two days."

I'd stood to pull the sweats all the way up, since that seemed to be the style nowadays, but I stopped and looked at him. "Two days?" I sank back onto the bed.

"Ruthie said it was the spell. It was very powerful."

"You spoke to Ruthie?"

"Yes. Annette panicked when she couldn't wake you and brought up the app. Or the file. Or the video chat. What is that, by the way?"

"No idea."

"Annette told us what happened. The gate? The floating woman?"

"Right. There was a microburst."

"Sweetheart, Ruthie tried to tell us how powerful you were, but we just had no idea."

"How did you do it?" Dad asked.

"I have no clue, guys. One minute I'm watching that poor woman fall to her death from outside the gate, and the next I'm inside with my arms up, holding her in midair, and there is no gate. It was like a dream. Or an acid trip. Or a Marvel movie."

"You're amazing, cariña."

"Beyond," Papi said.

I lowered my head. "I'm really not."

"It's about time." Annette walked in carrying my laptop. "Someone wants to see you." She cradled the thing like she was bringing a baby to a new mother. Then I realized Ink was on the keyboard. His tail draped over the side and swished back and forth in annoyance at having his throne moved. "He won't get off and I'm trying to talk to Ruthie."

Ah. She'd graduated from Mrs. Goode to Ruthie.

I scooched back on the bed, pulled Ink to me, and waved at my latest acquisition. "Hey, Gigi."

The pride in her eyes, I expected. The anger, not so much. "What were you thinking? Doing such a powerful spell like that so soon? You could've died, Defiance. I have half a mind to ground you."

The smile I fought won out in the end and spread across my face. "Thank you, grandma."

She raised a brow.

"Sorry. Gigi. Thank you."

"Oh." She waved a hand and looked away, the wetness in her eyes breaking free.

"For them," I said, pointing to my dads.

Papi took Dad's hand in his.

"For Percy."

She still didn't look at me.

"For keeping me alive."

"Barely." She finally turned back to me. "Barely, Defiance. Do you know what would happen if you hadn't made it?"

"Not really."

"My entire life would have been for naught. All the sacrifices I made. Not being able to watch you grow up."

"I'm sorry, Gigi."

She bent her head and put a hand over her eyes. After a moment, she removed it and said, "Also, I have never, in all of the thirty-nine years I walked the earth—"

Annette and I both giggled.

"—heard of anything so magnificent. So magical." She put a hand over her heart. "I didn't even know something like that was possible."

"Me neither," Annette said, leaning in for a high five.

"Did the chief tell you what happened?"

"And Annette."

Annette? My BFF was definitely moving up in the world. I was *this* close to legally changing her name to Nannette.

"Though neither seemed to have actually seen

anything, which is both frustrating and a relief. Hopefully no one else did either."

"I didn't do the spell on purpose, Gigi. It just kind of happened."

She shook her head. "I'm so honored, Defiance, to be a part of your life."

"Yep," Annette said, reaching over for a second high five, mostly because I had to lean forward and every movement I made annoyed Ink.

"As are we," my dads said.

"Let me get this straight," I said to them, "since we're on the subject. I was laying here, knocking on death's door, and you two went shopping for antiques?"

"Can you blame us?" Papi asked. "The stores here are to die for."

Speaking of knocks, someone was at the door downstairs. I got the feeling that was going to happen a lot.

"Got it!" Annette said and lumbered off the bed, shaking it as much as possible. Again, to annoy Ink.

"So," I said, biting a cuticle, "what do you guys think of Roane?"

Papi spoke first. "From Annette's description, he's a looker."

Dad agreed with a nod.

"Wait, you've been here two days and you haven't met him yet?"

They glanced at each other in question, both shaking their heads.

"Did he leave?" I asked Ruthie.

"Not that I know of, but I don't get out much, dear."

The fault line between my brows emerged.

"It's the bank robber guy," Annette said.

Mr. Bourne, a large man with exquisite skin, followed

her into the room. "Please excuse the interruption. I was in the neighborhood."

"That's okay. I meant to come by. Instead, I went into a short but strangely refreshing coma."

"I'm . . . sorry."

"Thanks. You were robbed?"

"I was never robbed, Ms. Dayne."

"But you said—"

"You said, actually." A grin played about his mouth. "I've been trying to get you to sign these papers for the last week."

"Oh, no." I waved an index finger. "I'm not signing anything else as long as I live."

"Trust me." He stepped forward. "You'll want to sign these."

Dad stood and took them from him.

"It's your account information, your signature card, and your bank card. I don't normally make house calls."

"I don't have an account with you, Mr. Bourne."

"No, but your grandmother did. I've been trying to tell you for days. She left you a sizable inheritance."

"I know. I've already signed the papers on the house."

"These papers are different."

I eyed him with as much suspicion as I could muster. "How different?"

"You're quite well off, Ms. Dayne."

"You're quite funny, Mr. Bourne." Though I did have a check for fifty grand burning a hole in my pocket. Not that I would dare count my chickens until it cleared.

"No, I mean it," he said to both me and my dads when they cast him a surprised expression. "I wouldn't normally say something this gauche, but to put it mildly, Ms. Dayne, you're rich."

I paused and gave him a good once over, trying to assess the state of his mental health. "No way."

"You're loaded."

"How loaded?"

"Mercedes S-Class loaded."

"Yes!" I threw my fist into the air in celebration. "I can buy another sandwich! Or," I said, my mind racing, "a lobster roll."

I looked down and realized Gigi was pretending to be on pause again, so I had to try not to laugh while mouthing the words, "Thank you."

Her pause face faltered and the barest hint of a grin shined through.

"So, I take it we're staying?" Annette asked me after everyone left. My dads went to get takeout from Dube's. I'd heard they had great seafood. Good thing because my stomach was singing the song of her people.

I shrugged. "Welcome to Massachusetts."

"Yes," she said. "Are those my sweats?"

SIXTEEN

If he eats French fries with a fork,
he's probably not going to do that
thing you like with his tongue.
-True fact

I decided to storm the dungeons and invite Roane up to dinner. He hadn't surfaced in two days. That worried me.

Though the stairs creaked as I stepped down them, the basement itself was much brighter than I thought it would be. The last steps ended in an open commons area with three heavy doors on three distressed walls. Plaster and paint had cracked and peeled to reveal beautiful stonework underneath. Like a treasure just waiting to be uncovered, and I couldn't help but wonder if someone distressed the walls on purpose.

I tried the thick wooden door on the left first. It was clearly Ruthie's magic room. I inched inside, the musty basement scent giving way to the aroma of dried plants and rich oils. My fingers brushed across a light switch on the wall closest to me. I flipped it. Instead of an incandescent bulb lighting the room, a series of gas lanterns on the walls flickered to life, their flames creating a soft glow.

Bunches of greenery hung drying upside down from a clothesline overhead. Dozens of jars of herbs and flowers and eyes of newt lined the walls with utensils and a work area in the center. I half expected to see a cauldron for boil and bubble. Instead, it was more medicinal, like an alchemist's pharmacy from the sixteenth century.

I turned out the lanterns—something I never thought I'd do—and tried the middle door. It was locked, so I assumed that one was Roane's apartment and went to check out the one on the right before invading his space.

The heavy door, identical to the first two, swung wide and I stepped inside an apartment any New Yorker would've been proud to call home. It was modern and luxurious like a penthouse on Fifth Avenue.

"Hello?" I said softly. When I didn't get an answer, I continued deeper inside.

Blacks blended into grays, but the color scheme was where any resemblance to the rest of the house ended. This was a contemporary designer's dream. Clean. Well-lit. Sharp lines, industrial touches, and stainless appliances.

I walked through slowly, taking in what was essentially Roane. Had he decorated it? Or remodeled it? Was this his design? If so, he took the label of journeyman to a whole new level.

After a search of a bedroom off to the side that had the same rugged, industrial feel punctuated with slate blues and hazelnut, I went into the living room. The light from the kitchen barely filtered this far, and I didn't want to turn on the floor lamp on my right. I was trying not to actually touch anything since I was essentially breaking and entering. He clearly wasn't here.

Maybe, just this once, I could . . .

I cast an illumination spell. It vibrated along my fingers and cast a soft glow that filled the room. I looked at the old maps he had on his walls, the stacks of books on the floor, and the furniture that looked straight out of a design magazine. And atop one particular piece of furniture lay a sensuous creature of both Celtic and Viking descent.

Even asleep, Roane radiated a soft, quiet kind of danger. His sculpted body lay prone across the couch. He wore jeans, no less, cut low on his hips, his bare feet hanging off the edge. The scars on his left ankle almost visible. His hands were clasped at this stomach. His tattoo-covered chest bare. It rose and fell in an even rhythm.

Ink had found his way downstairs and was sprawled on his shoulder against the sofa back, his head snuggled against Roane's cheek. The sweetness level in the room skyrocketed, making the man even sexier. A feat I didn't think possible.

Seeing them together at last debunked my whole shapeshifter theory. Which, in the grand scheme of things, had been an odd thing to think in the first place.

I didn't dare wake him. I did, however, want to commemorate the moment. Or just be a total perv. Either way.

In my defense concerning the sin I was about to commit, the total disrespect for his privacy, he was a work of art. The hills and valleys covered in ink. The perfect lines of his face. The smooth stubble framing a chiseled mouth. And his hands. Holy heaven. Large and strong and yet somehow elegant.

After wrangling my phone out of a pocket in the sweat pants, I opened the camera app and held it up to him.

Without opening his eyes, he asked, "Are you taking my picture?"

I almost dropped the phone. Well, I did drop it, then I spent the next thirty seconds trying to catch it, only to swat it away and send it crashing against his wall. I hurried to pick it up, cooing and stroking it. Trying to convince us both it would be okay.

Once I had it firmly in my grasp, I turned back to him. "What? No. And unless you can see through your eyelids, you have no proof."

"Ink told me. He's like a bodyguard."

"He's like an asshole."

"That too. Want to join me?"

He had yet to open his eyes. That was a good thing, because those shimmering olive irises had superpowers. They sapped my strength and siphoned my brain cells faster than a gang of frat boys could siphon a keg.

Despite every atom in my body screaming to do otherwise, I said, "I'm okay here."

He finally lifted his lids and, just as I suspected, my brain disappeared. His gaze traveled over me. That was okay, though. My gaze traveled over him, as well.

"You slept for a long time," he said.

"Yes, and that's the last time I prick my finger on a spindle. Who knew curses were a real thing?"

Trying not to disturb Ink, he scooted out from under him and rose to get a shirt. I fought a wave of depression over that fact.

When he turned his back to me, I looked at the tattoo there. At the symbol etched over an early map of Salem. At the spell.

I stepped to him and lifted my hand to touch it. To smooth my fingers over the lines, the contact like closing an electrical current.

How did he know what this was? Or did he?

He straightened when my fingers touched the tattoo. Stilled. Looked at me through his periphery from over his shoulder.

"Do you know what this is?" I asked.

After a moment, he answered. "Yes."

"How?"

He dropped his gaze to the shirt in his hands. "Something that happened a long time ago."

Then I noticed he had a bandage wrapped around his lower waist where he'd had his hands clasped. I scanned the living room a little closer now that my eyes had adjusted. Bloody bandages filled a small trash can and lay on the coffee table in front of the sofa along with a bottle of hydrogen peroxide and pain pills.

Alarm raced over my skin. "What happened?"

"Nothing. I slipped while using a paint scraper and paid the price."

My hand drifted down to his right side. His injured side. I knew not only where the wound was, but how it got there.

Yet how did I know?

Then it hit me. When he'd turned toward me after I'd fired the gun. The wolf. Olive green eyes almost glowing.

I backed away from him. My mind had somehow settled on *shapeshifter* even when I thought magic and witches and spells complete fiction. Somewhere in the back of my mind the truth sat hidden.

He didn't look at me for a long moment as I stood there absorbing the facts. Trying to make sense of them.

I decided to start with the simplest question. "How do you know that spell?"

His jaw worked as he bit down. After a long moment, he finally answered. "Because you used it to find me when we were kids."

I swayed slightly and had to brace my palm against a wall. "You were the boy in the video," I said, my lungs struggling for air. "The one who was missing. But the woman, your mother, had a different last name."

"As did I. She changed both our names after my father was convicted of attempted murder."

I covered my mouth and said from behind it, "He was going to kill you."

"Yes."

"Okay. Okay, I get that, but how, Roane, are you a shapeshifter?"

He laughed softly and shook his head, preparing to deny it.

"How are you a wolf?"

Unable to make sense of his T-shirt, he tossed it across the room then strode to his kitchen, took out a bottle of beer, and downed it. He took out another and leveled an expression on me that could only be described as distrustful.

Because I was onto him? Because I'd figured it out?

I'd seen him in my dreams days before I saw him in real life. It was as though the minute Ruthie passed away, the minute her protection spell was broken, all of this knowledge came back to me. I just had to pry most of it out.

"You saved my life," I said.

His shimmering gaze studied me as he took another swig.

"I would be dead if not for you. As would Annette and Sara. Wade would have killed us all."

"Yeah, well, you saved mine first."

He slammed the bottle on the counter and walked into his bedroom. I heard the shower come on and I followed the sound. He was angry, though I didn't think that anger was directed at me. Or, at least, not solely at me.

His jeans lay on the floor and he stood with a towel around his hips in the bathroom trying to remove the blood-soaked bandage.

"Did you go to the hospital?"

He scoffed. "Don't you mean the vet?"

"Roane." I stepped to him.

He kept working on the bandage furiously.

"I'm staying," I said. "I'm going to live here."

"Good for you. Unfortunately, I'm not. It's time I move on."

I realized he was not angry but embarrassed. Why else behave this way from my figuring out his secret?

He tugged too hard on the bandage and ripped his wound open. "Fuck." He threw tattered gauze in the trash, dropped the towel, and strode into the shower. It was the kind that had two staggered rock walls instead of a shower door.

I took Annette's sweats off so I wouldn't drench them, then entered the exquisite thing with only a T-shirt and my underwear.

He stood leaning against the wall, one arm braced above his head, water cascading down his magnificent back and over his steely buttocks.

"Let me look," I said, this time with more authority.

It didn't work. He didn't move. He just let the water drain the blood off his wound, which was on his side below his ribcage and above his hip.

The cut was narrow but deep. I'd watched in horror as the knife sank into his flesh.

"You need stitches."

"I need you to leave."

Out of respect for his wishes, I would leave. Before I did, however, I stepped closer. Ignoring the splash of water, I raised my hand and drew a spell on his skin over the wound. His muscles bunched and he sucked in a sharp breath through his teeth. I sealed the wound then turned to leave him alone.

"It's not healed," I said just before stepping out. "It's only closed. It'll still take time to heal." I walked out of the stall.

His words stopped me. "I'm not the boy."

After pivoting back to him, I stood on the threshold. "I don't understand."

He raked a hand through his wet hair, the red even darker now. "The boy died."

Trying to grasp his meaning, I asked, "The boy I found in the video?"

"Yes."

"But you *are* the boy I found in the video. That's the symbol. You said I saved your life."

"Mine. Not the boy's."

"Roane, I don't understand." I grabbed a towel and went back in.

He turned off the water and accepted it, but he wouldn't look at me, his normally hawklike gaze nowhere in sight.

He didn't use the towel on himself, however. Water had splashed onto my arms and face. He lifted it, looking up at last through spiked lashes, and blotted the water off my cheeks and mouth.

His nearness warmed me even more than the steam and scalding water had.

"Your grandmother begged me to go," he said, paying careful attention to my mouth, brushing the cloth softly across my lips. "I didn't want to interfere with your life, Defiance, but she said you were in trouble. How could I not go?"

"You mean with Wade Scott? In the woods?"

He nodded.

I took the towel and gave him the same careful attention, patting the stubble on his face. Brushing it across his mouth. He moved closer and the animal magnetism part of his personality made so much more sense now.

"How is this possible?" I asked. "These things are myth. Legend. Fabricated stories to scare children into obedience. Yet everything I've been taught was not real is coming to life before my eyes. How?"

"You were born of royal blood," he said, as though that explained everything.

"Let's put me aside for a moment because you are much, much more interesting.

His jaw flexed. He took back the towel, wrapped it around his lean waist, and stepped around me. "I'm not nearly as interesting as you might imagine."

"I don't know," I said, following him. "You do shapeshift into a wolf. That's pretty freaking interesting. But what I'm most interested in right now is, how are you not the boy? Was there another boy who looked exactly like the missing boy just hanging out, hoping my magics would find him?"

Ink hopped onto the sink. Roane turned on the faucet, just barely, so the adorably mangy cat could use it as his personal water fountain.

"I saw the spell in my mind's eye," he explained. "The symbol you drew, hot and bright and comforting."

I leaned on the sink next to him.

"I was in the cabin with him. The boy. The real Roane. I'd been caught in one of Huber's traps. Of course, I didn't know that at the time. I didn't know what it was or who'd set it. I just knew I'd been trapped and was in tremendous pain."

Alarm shot through me. I tried not to let it show. Not to ruin the moment. He was opening up at last. I couldn't let this opportunity slip away. "Trapped how?"

He looked down and watched Ink lap at the water, but his gaze slid past him. "Steel. The kind that snaps shut."

I squeezed my lids together. "Like an animal trap?" Who would put a child in an animal trap?

"You know how they say an animal will chew through its leg to get out of one? I tried. But he found me before I could manage it."

The world tilted as the image of him caught in a trap formed in my mind, and then it hit me. As unfathomable and incomprehensible and inconceivable as it was, it hit me. "You were a wolf," I said. It was not a question.

"A cub. A few months old. Huber didn't care. He picked up the trap and dragged me by my broken leg across the rough terrain and through ice-cold water to his cabin."

I tried to keep my breathing steady. To show no reaction.

"He had lots of dead animals. Carcasses hanging in various states of mutilation."

The image, and the thought of him being there, blurred the edges of my vision.

"But the boy was already dead when your magics found us. When they sought him out and found me instead. I knew I was about to die, too, but then I saw the symbol and your warmth washed over me and I realized I had a chance to survive. So I . . . I became him." He hit me with a feverish glint, as though pleading with me to understand.

It pierced my heart.

"Huber was busy digging a grave for the boy, so I scrambled under a cot. And he buried him, Roane, right in the middle of the cabin. Right there beside me."

He was lost in the story. I was horrified by it.

"Then he picked up the chain to the trap and tried to pull me out from under the bed."

Heartbroken.

"He didn't know what I'd become and, thankfully, he never found out. The police busted down the door. When they found me hiding under the cot, they didn't look any farther."

Devastated.

"Your magics transformed me. They allowed me to become him. I don't know how, really. It just happened."

My magics. Were they really that powerful? "So, when the police found you, you were essentially a newborn."

He lifted a shoulder in bashful agreement.

"Is that why you didn't talk until you were seven?"

He shook his head. "I picked up the language fast enough. Another byproduct of your magics would be my guess. I just didn't have anything to say. I only started talking when your grandmother found me."

"Ruthie?"

"I'd run away from home." He ducked his head, a pink hue blossoming on his cheeks, and I found it the most endearing thing I'd ever seen. "From Roane's home. His mother's adoration was a lot. She never knew I wasn't really her son. That he was buried and forgotten in her ex's cabin. Sometimes I just couldn't take it. I had to get away."

I wanted to wrap my arms around him, though I doubted he'd appreciate it at the moment. "I understand that kind of pressure. It's not your fault that you needed space."

"Your grandmother used a spell to find me, only she came to get me herself. No one else. She told me she knew the truth. She knew what I was."

"She knew?" I straightened and pushed off the sink. "Why didn't she tell me?"

"I asked her not to. It's a lot to take in. I didn't . . . I'd hoped you wouldn't find out."

"Why?"

He practically gawked at me. "Are you understanding what I am?"

"I understand that you are the most amazing thing I've ever met."

If I knew the truth about him, it was only fair that he knew the truth about me. I am a sucker for the underdog. I cared about nothing else. He could've told me he was from Krypton and I would've fallen, just like I was doing right then and there.

"Wait," I sobered and thought back. "You said *three*. You said my magics found the three of you. Do you mean Huber?"

He shook his head then gestured toward the cat that'd apparently been really thirsty.

I gaped at him. "Ink? He was there, too?"

"Huber had him in a cage. I don't know if he was his pet or what."

I picked Ink up. Poor scraggly guy.

Roane rubbed under his chin. "He was the only other

creature alive in the cabin when your magics engulfed us. They suffused us both." His gaze met mine. "Changed us both. In very different ways, of course."

I lowered Ink onto the counter and did the math. Granted, not my strongest area. "Roane, that was over forty years ago."

"Exactly." He nodded and ran a strong hand over the cat's back. It arched in response before he decided to swat the water with his paw. "We've been through a lot together."

"I'd say so." I couldn't get past one aspect of his story. "When they found you, were you still in the trap?"

"I was." He showed me his ankle, the mangled scars. The straight lines where they'd clearly done surgery. "They didn't take the trap off until we got to the hospital for fear an artery was severed." He stopped and grinned at me. "It was a long trip."

"I'm so sorry, Roane. I mean, is that what you've continued to go by?"

"Yes. In honor of my human mother. I went back, years later, and dug up my brother's bones."

"Your brother?"

"Roane. The first Roane. I began seeing him as a brother. As a member of my pack who didn't make it."

"I love that. It's very . . . honorable."

"I buried him with our mother when she died twenty years later of cancer." The loss stung. His eyes watered despite his best efforts. "She was a good person. She deserved to have her real son back."

I ached to touch him. He was so close. So magnetic.

He tilted his head. "Have I lost you completely, Ms. Dayne?"

I blinked back to reality. "Do you think I'm that easily frightened, Mr. Wildes?"

My phone dinged. I reached down and dug it out of the sweatpants I'd discarded on the floor. "Dinner's here. Will you join us?"

He withdrew immediately. "I'm okay."

I got the feeling he was quite the loner. This could be a tough sell. "Roane, please join us. I told my dads what you did when my ex and the monster-in-law showed up. They're dying to meet you."

He let out a sigh, looked down at the towel, and asked, "Do I have to get dressed?"

"Not at all. Annette would probably appreciate it more if you didn't." I knew I would.

I picked up the sweats and put them back on. When I stood, I realized he'd been watching me in the mirror. So I thought it only fair to watch him dress.

Then he dropped the towel and I took note of just how gifted he truly was, I got flustered and hurried out to wait for him in his living room.

I hadn't even scratched the surface of all the questions I had. What was it like to suddenly become human? How did he learn our social norms? How did he and Ink find each other again after the rescue?

So many questions, but I was staying. We were all staying. We had time.

SEVENTEEN

One day I was born.
Then everything bothered me.
And that brings us up to date.
-Defiance Dayne: A Memoir

Who knew my life could change so much after forty?

We had dinner and Roane, even reserved, was quite the hit. Speaking of which, how did he master English better than most native speakers? Did he have a language before becoming human? Was there a secret wolf language?

I started making a list on my phone of all the questions I had, because this was happening. I had a werewolf living in my basement. What a strange week.

"We could've called it A&D Ointment," Annette said from beside me. We'd gone to bed late and yet we still couldn't sleep. Of course, I'd been asleep for two days. "You know, because we're like a salve for the soul. Annette and Defiance. Unfortunately, it's already taken."

"Darn. Good one, though." She was killing me, going on and on about our business. What to call it. Should we get a sign? The neighbors would love that. "Still, I'm thinking my initial should come first."

"You're probably right," she said, scrunching her nose in thought.

"I like to think I am."

"So, you were both wet when you came up to dinner. Together. All wet and glowy."

"I keep telling you, I forgot my shine-free powder."

She turned onto her side and watched me as I studied Ruthie's journal and tried to ignore the fact that she'd turned onto her side and was watching me.

"What?" I asked at last.

"Deets, baby. You can't leave me hanging."

I giggled. "Nothing happened." I didn't tell her about the werewolf thing, and I wouldn't until I had his permission.

"You were wet."

I shrugged.

"He was wet."

Another helpless shrug.

She set her jaw. "I didn't want to have to do this, but I will take matters into my own hands."

"Yeah?"

"I'm not afraid to be cruel."

"Sounds kinky."

"First, I will turn on the lights while you're sleeping."

"No," I said with a gasp.

"Every night."

"How will I survive?"

"I will eviscerate your biorhythm."

"What has my biorhythm ever done to you?"

"Then—and remember, you're practically forcing me to do this—I will prank call all of the boys you had crushes on in high school."

"All thirty-seven of them?" We went to a great school. Our cup of hotties had runneth over.

"From *your* phone."

"You wouldn't."

"I would. You know I would."

She would.

"There's one thing we never got around to doing," she said, changing the subject.

"Playing with Dana's wieners?"

"Four words."

"Playing with Dana's wieners," I repeated, more insistent that time.

"Explore the secret passageway."

"Oh, yeah. I forgot about that." I didn't. I thought about that passageway every time I was in the shower. Naked. And alone. I'd have to make sure the shelves locked from the inside.

Annette's voice grew softer. "This house is basically my ideal heaven."

"Dark and dreary?"

"Eclectic and bold and achingly beautiful."

Couldn't argue with that.

"I think I want to die here."

"No."

She had no comeback for that bit of stellar articulation. Who could blame her?

Two minutes later, the girl who had way too much excited energy to even consider sleeping was snoring softly into her pillow. I thought about seeing what Ruthie was up to. We didn't get to talk much after dinner, and I had questions for her, too. Oddly enough, they all centered on a certain hot shapeshifter.

Instead, I focused on unlocking her book of shadows. It was strange. I could only unlock certain words or phrases. I couldn't help but wonder if she'd done it that way on purpose.

I finally became frustrated enough to reveal the entire book in one fell swoop. No more of this page at a time crap. The read was well worth the shock I'd received doing it.

It went back to the time when she met Percy. How handsome he was. How dangerous. At least I knew my tastes were inherited. Or maybe it was just a girl thing. The dream of reforming a bad boy.

I skipped ahead to when I was born. Ruthie hadn't exaggerated. My birth caused something of a stir in the witch community. As fun as it was to read about me, I wanted to know more about my mother.

I skimmed Ruthie's beautiful handwriting until I'd come across my mother's name: Pania Goode. Then I'd soak it up. Her childhood. Her first spells. Her biggest mistakes. Her greatest accomplishments.

According to Gigi, my mother was too much like her father, Percy. She was the definition of a witch gone bad. Partying. Sleeping around—gasp! Performing spells she had no right performing.

Then I was born and everything changed. Either my mother changed or Ruthie did. Either way, something was different.

I'd wanted kids at one time, not that motherhood had ever been my life's goal.

Or had it? I'd practically begged Kyle. I was running low on impregnable egg sacs, as I liked to call them. Mostly because I was a romantic. He'd never wanted kids. I'd known that going into the marriage. It was not my place to try to change his mind and it was unfair for me to expect something that hadn't been part of the bargain. Then again, he turned out to be a conniving dick, so . . .

Now, however, it looked like it would never happen. There was always adoption. I'd been adopted. Of course, who knew if I'd be as lucky as my dads had been.

I giggled at my own joke—those two never stood a chance—trying not to wake the beast beside me. Unless one had coffee in one's hand, one did everything in one's power not to wake the sleeping dragon. Wine worked, too.

The more I read, the more I realized what a handful my mother was. Yet Ruthie's love for the woman who bore me shined through on every page.

Surprisingly, I turned to the last page in the book. I figured there'd be more about my dads and how they met and the adoption process, but it ended with one line that . . .

Odd.

It had a shape drawn over and over on the page. A spell. And it looked like a child had drawn it. I realized it was the spell Ruthie had drawn and asked me about earlier. The reveal spell. The one that exposed the betrayal of a loved one or a friend.

Ruthie had written over the drawings, and I struggled to read it. After I managed it, I read it again. Thought about it. Mulled it over. Read it a third time. And a fourth.

Then it hit me. Goose bumps sprouted over my skin and my fingers itched to do a spell. I could see how spellcasting could become addictive.

Anger slowly engulfed me. I tore the page out of the book and went downstairs to where my laptop sat charging. The more I thought about it, the clearer it became, until I stood in front of the laptop, fury swirling around me.

Ruthie was conveniently absent. The entire screen was an endless white.

"Ruthie!" I said, trying to get her attention.

She appeared as though out of a mist.

"Is this true?" I asked, jutting the page toward the screen. My fury was gaining mass. It caused my hair to stand on end.

She knew exactly what I was talking bout. "We can discuss this when you've had some sleep."

"No, we can't." And as though of their own accord, my fingers drew a spell on the air and my palm pushed it into the veil. It searched like a hunter in the night.

Percy shivered and Ink hissed then ran for cover. I could hardly blame them. I'd lit up the entire kitchen with a spell I could never have imagined existed.

Then Ruthie materialized before me in her cream-colored dress. She whirled to face me. Patted herself. Stared at me, her blue eyes huge. "Defiance—"

"Is it true?" I asked again over the cyclone now swirling around us.

Her blond hair whipped about her face. Her dress flew around her. "Defiance, how did you that?"

I stepped to her, my anger barely contained, and asked one last time, "Is it true?"

"I don't know what you mean," she lied, yelling above the wind.

Annette rushed in. My dads followed. And lastly, Roane. The commotion must've woken them. Either that or Percy did. Now Roane would get to see me at my worst.

Annette and my dads stood terrified. Roane was . . . resigned.

I gaped at him. He knew. After all that talk about his human mother, he knew the truth about mine.

"How many people have you killed?" I asked Ruthie over the roar.

She lifted her chin a visible notch. "I've killed three men. I told you."

I practically growled at her and stepped closer. "That's not what I asked. How many people have you killed? Not men. People."

She lowered her head and the winds died down and she said softly, "Four."

I covered my mouth with a shaking hand and reread the lines.

She's gone. I had no choice. May the great goddess embrace her soul.

"Ruthie, did you—" I stopped to swallow, my throat having suddenly gone dry "—did you kill my mother?"

After an eternity of absolute silence, she raised her lashes, and said softly, "Yes."

THANK YOU!!!

Thank you for reading **BETWIXT: A PARANORMAL WOMEN'S FICTION NOVEL (BETWIXT & BETWEEN BOOK 1**). We hope you enjoyed it! If you liked this book – or any of Darynda's other releases – please consider rating the book at the online retailer of your choice. Your ratings and reviews help other readers find new favorites, and of course there is no better or more appreciated support for an author than word of mouth recommendations from happy readers. Thanks again for your interest in Darynda's books!

If you liked BETWIXT, you are going to love the second installment of Defiance's story: BEWITCHED!

Forty-something Defiance Dayne only recently discovered she comes from a long line of powerful witches. Added to that was the teensy, infinitesimal fact that she is what's called a charmling. One of three on the entire planet. And there are other witches who will stop at nothing to steal her

immense power, which would basically involve her unfortunate and untimely death.

No one told her life after forty would mean having to learn
new lifeskills—such as how to dodge supernatural assassins
while casting from a moving vehicle—or that the sexiest
man alive would be living in her basement.

Whoever said life begins at forty was clearly a master of the
underappreciated and oft maligned understatement.

Darynda Jones
   www.daryndajones.com

ALSO BY DARYNDA JONES

**Never miss a new book
from Darynda Jones!**

Sign up for Darynda's newsletter!

**Be the first to get notified of new releases and be
eligible for special subscribers-only exclusive
content and giveaways. Sign up today**!

Also from DARYNDA JONES

(click to purchase)

PARANORMAL

BEWTIXT & BETWEEN

Betwixt

Bewitched

Beguiled

CHARLEY DAVIDSON SERIES

First Grave on the Right

For I have Sinned: A Charley Short Story

Second Grave on the Left

Third Grave Dead Ahead

Fourth Grave Beneath my Feet

Fifth Grave Past the Light

Sixth Grave on the Edge

Seventh Grave and No Body

Eight Grave After Dark

Brighter than the Sun: A Reyes Novella

The Dirt on Ninth Grave

The Curse of Tenth Grave

Eleventh Grave in Moonlight

The Trouble with Twelfth Grave

Summoned to Thirteenth Grave

The Graveyard Shift: A Charley Novella

THE NEVERNEATH

A Lovely Drop

The Monster

Dust Devils: A Short Story of The NeverNeath

MYSTERY

SUNSHINE VICRAM SERIES

A Bad Day for Sunshine

YOUNG ADULT

DARKLIGHT SERIES

Death and the Girl Next Door

Death, Doom, and Detention

Death and the Girl he Loves

SHORT STORIES

Want more Paranormal Women's Fiction? Check out Robyn Peterman's IT'S A WONDERFUL MIDLIFE CRISIS!

Whoever said life begins at forty must have been heavily medicated, drunk, or delusional.

Thirty-nine was a fantastic year. I was married to the man I loved. I had a body that worked without creaking. My grandma, who raised me, was still healthy, and life was pretty damned good.

But as *they* say, all good things come to an end. I'd honestly love to know who '*they*' are and rip them a new one.

One year later, I'm a widow. My joints are starting to ache. Gram is in the nursing home, and dead people think my home is some kind of supernatural bed and breakfast. Gluing body parts onto semi-transparent people has become a side job—deceased people I'm not even sure are actually there. I think they need my help, but since I don't speak *dead*, we're having a few issues.

To add to the heap of trouble, there's a new dangerously smokin' hot lawyer at the firm who won't stop giving me the eye. My BFF is

thrilled with her new frozen face, thanks to her plastic surgeon, her alimony check, and the miracle of Botox. And then there's the little conundrum that I'm becoming way too attached to my ghostly squatters... Like Cher, I'd like to turn back time. Now.

No can do.

Whatever. I have wine, good friends, and an industrial sized box of superglue. What could possibly go wrong?

Everything, apparently.

All in all, it's shaping up to be a wonderful midlife crisis...

BUY LINK

https://robynpeterman.com/its-a-wonderful-midlife-crisis/

MORE PARANORMAL WOMEN'S FICTION

Still need more Paranormal Women's Fiction to tide you over? You can check out more of the amazing authors in the genre at:

www.paranormalwomensfiction.net

You will find fantastic books by my buddies; Robyn Peterman, Mandy M. Roth, Michelle M. Pillow, Shannon Mayer, K.F. Breene, Jana DeLeon, Denise Grover Swank, Eve Langlais, Kristen Painter, Deanna Chase, Elizabeth Hunter and Christine Bell!

ACKNOWLEDGMENTS

Most people believe writing is a solitary venture and, well, much of it is. However, getting a book ready to be unleashed upon an unsuspecting world is not. I must thank a few people without whom this book would've sucked.

First, as always, my amazing assistants, Netters and Dana. The lurves of my life. The sparkles of my eye. The thumps of my heart.

The incredible talent behind the editing process, Trayce Layne, who did hours of reading and research and developmental editing, and Casey Harris-Parks at Heart Full of Ink, who came through with flying colors in my hour of need with a last-minute rush to the finish line. Thank you, guys, so much!

Robyn Peterman who held my hand during this whole process, as indie publishing is like a hostile planet onto which I've crash-landed. I'm still getting my bearings, dodging enemy fire, and learning the finer points of formatting.

Joe and Jennifer Settle for answering my dumb questions. (Yes, they actually exist. Dumb questions. Though Joe and Jennifer exist, too.)

My beloved Grimlets, for the same reason. I hope your opinion of me has not lessened. I really did have a literary rationale for asking the things I did. Except for that one question about chocolate covered strawberries. That was purely personal.

To my amazing family for understanding why I walked around with bloodshot eyes and zero sense of space and time while writing this. You are everything.

And thank you so much to the Paranormal Women's Fiction group, the Fab 13, for allowing me admittance into the coolest club around and the opportunity to share in this great adventure. Without you, I would still be twiddling my thumbs, saying to myself, "I should really try indie." Thanks for the push. And the support. You're like a push-up bra without the uncomfortable repercussions.

And thank you, dear reader, for choosing this book and allowing Defiance, Annette, Ruthie, and Roane into your lives. I hope you grow to love them as much as I do.

ABOUT THE AUTHOR

New York Times and *USA Today* Bestselling Author Darynda Jones has won numerous awards for her work, including a prestigious RITA®, a Golden Heart®, and a Daphne du Maurier, and her books have been translated into17 languages. As a born storyteller, she grew up spinning tales of dashing damsels and heroes in distress for any unfortunate soul who happened by. Darynda lives in the Land of Enchantment, also known as New Mexico, with her husband and two beautiful sons, the Mighty, Mighty Jones Boys.

Connect with Darynda online:

www.DaryndaJones.com

CPSIA information can be obtained
at www.ICGtesting.com
Printed in the USA
BVHW030237160420
577720BV00001B/176

9 781734 385212